*Also by* Steven Key Meyers

**Novels**

*That's My Story*

*Save the Max Man!*

*Family Romance*

*My Mad Russian: Three Tales*

*Queer's Progress*

*Springtime in Siena*

*All That Money*

*Good People*

**Nonfiction**

*The Man in the Balloon:
Harvey Joiner's Wondrous 1877*

**Plays**

*A Journal of the Plague Year,
and Other Plays and Adaptations*

# *The* Wedding *on* Big Bone Hill

A Novel

Steven Key Meyers

*The Wedding on Big Bone Hill*

Copyright © 2021 Steven Key Meyers
All rights reserved.

ISBN 978-1-7368333-7-7

Published by Steven Key Meyers/The Smash-and-Grab Press

All rights reserved. No part of this publication may be reproduced, stored in a retrieval system or transmitted in any form or by any means, electronic, mechanical, recording or otherwise, without the prior written permission of the author.

The characters appearing in this work are fictitious. Any resemblance to real persons, living or dead, is coincidental.

*The Wedding on Big Bone Hill* was originally published by BookLocker in 2014, and *Junkie, Indiana* was originally published by BookLocker in 2015. Both have been revised for this edition.

# SMASH
# & GRAB press

The Wedding on Big Bone Hill    3

Junkie, Indiana    125

# The Wedding on Big Bone Hill

*Another, gratefully,
for my father,
Harold Burton Meyers*

Hell is always at hand, which you cannot say of heaven.

Akira Kurosawa<br>*Ran*

Then I saw that there was a way to hell, even from the gates of heaven.

John Bunyan<br>*Pilgrim's Progress*

## 1.

ANY NUMBER of websites cater to the recreational-vehicle community, gaudy advocates of *vanlife* and the *RV lifestyle*. Many offer all manner of classified ads, running the gamut from *rigs for sale* to *employment opportunities*. Those vying for notice in the latter category generally seek *workampers*—in RV parlance, *volunteers*—to perform maintenance tasks in local, state or national parks, be it mowing or cleaning restrooms or greeting the public, in return for—in lieu of salary—an RV site with water and power.

At *Wheels-Ho.com* in the winter of 2002/03 there appeared an ad that didn't particularly stand out from many similar ones:

> Wanted: couples/singles to work entrance booth, Fort Horace State Park, Kansas, Fri or share Sat/Sun, April thru Sept. Free site w/ water & elec. Email: Dennis33@flatlander-rfd.net

It was only in March—with America poised to invade Iraq and give Saddam Hussein the licking it forgot to give him in 1991—that Jack saw the ad. He was perusing the Web from the public library in the little Texas town where he'd parked his motorhome in November. He'd lived in the rig for a year and was finding the isolation of the RV lifestyle an engulfment it might be best to resist.

He thought, too, that an RV job might be fun as he continued his quest for Paradise, U.S.A.

Googling Fort Horace State Park, he found endless accounts of fishing and camping—it had a huge lake, thanks to an Army Corps of Engineers dam—plus myriad photographs of meadows, woods, a vast campground and especially of Big Bone Hill, that landmark of northeastern Kansas.

He wrote:

> Hi Dennis,
> Do you still need someone for your booth? I'm a single guy with a dog (she doesn't bite) in a 21-foot motorhome, headed north from the Texas hill country. A summer job's just what I'm looking for. Please let me know if I should come by Fort Horace State Park.
> Sincerely,
> Jack

Returning to the library the next day, he found a response sent not half an hour after his message:

> Hi Jack,
> Sure! Still have the Friday slot to fill—noon to 9:00, hour off for dinner—though there's a couple on board now for Sat/Sun. My first year as Vendor, appreciate your help! Season opens soon, so great to hear from you!
> Thanks,
> Dennis
> PS Your dog will love it!

All that enthusiasm made Jack a little wary. Still, he replied:

> Sounds good. If all goes well, I'll swing by in about a week. Let's meet before finalizing things?

He began seeing to his rig and taking Lady, his black Lab mix, on farewell walks along the Blanco River and through the town, so hospitable and pleasant over the mild winter. Already hints abounded that by summer Texas would be ablaze.

At his last library visit, the day before he started a leisurely drive northward, he found another email from Dennis, sent one night at 2:00 a.m.:

> Googled you, great to meet one of the FAMILY!
> Love the glam! PS What RU wearing?

All right, Jack thought, OK. He knew just the photographs Dennis had come upon, taken years earlier at a glam-rock Halloween party at the Hollywood LGBT drop-in center he and his dead lover attended, they with others caught in satirical gold-lamé that rayed out from outrageous lumps between their legs, below big eyes, big pouts and big hair.

What struck him now was how *young* were the boys in the pictures. But it's irritating, too, to be forever cute on the Internet when cuteness has faded past recall and the outrageousness of your crotch was anyway largely due to a sock.

## 2.

DONNA STOPPED OFF at the Fort Horace ranger station on her way to work the lunch shift at Long John Silver's. Entering to a jangle of bells, she told her Dad, standing at the counter in front of the wall of caged reptiles, that she was going to marry his boss.

Listening, Percy Bratcher treated his daughter to the sneer and flipping back of his unlikely ginger thatch that he bestowed so freely on the public. In fact, she had to break off when one of the off-season trickle of campers stepped in to ask for a map to the park. Flipping his hair, Percy with curled lip informed him they were out. The camper left and Donna resumed, flashing a ring that Percy thought sparkled grudgingly.

She lived with Mark, the wonder was that he would propose. After fleeing with her mother and brother the first time Percy got out of prison, she'd returned after his second stretch, the embodiment of the court's mercy in granting custody to a reformed and remorseful father. Naturally the head ranger fell for her.

"Married, huh?" Percy grunted. "He's a dog, you OK with that?"

Mark's affairs—besides those with park visitors, towns-women and outlying farm wives—included the one with Donna's mother that led to the standoff that landed Percy in prison in the first place.

"He's changed," Donna informed him. "Turning 40. Wants to settle down, raise a family."

"Sure," said Percy. "And you're—?"

"Nineteen in July." Which would also be the anniversary of her moving in with Mark (Percy didn't care to revisit that battle). She turned to leave, opened the door without jangling the bells. "Don't fuck it up, Daddy: Wasn't easy. Hey, it's *Kansas*. Been legal since I was twelve years old."

"Set a date?"

"Saturday of Labor Day weekend, on top of Big Bone Hill. Not too bad: the dress, cake, rent a shelter for the reception. But if you don't want to pay for it, we'll elope."

"Won't get off that easy," Percy growled at her departing yellow ruffles.

He watched her reach inside her ancient one-eyed Isuzu and

open the door. Duct tape held on the front bumper and propped up its remaining headlight, brightened the smashed-up fenders and secured the back window's plastic. A bungee cord closed the hood.

After she drove off he returned to arranging the morrow's annual springtime burn of Big Bone Hill.

At 4:59—he was nothing if not punctual—Percy wished the snakes and turtles goodnight, turned off the shortwave and the lights, locked the door and climbed, groaning, into his decommissioned park truck. It still had the siren and amber roof lights, but its insignia were painted out in a darker shade of brown than the rest.

He drove down the lane opposite the ranger station towards the swimming beach, but short of it turned into the woods where his old Airstream nestled against a slope like an undiscovered plane crash.

Indoors he sat down heavily and with his inevitable groan. His pet squirrel, Rocky, glad to see him, ran over and jumped in his lap. Percy, in no mood, brushed him off. In the process Rocky nipped his finger. Two telltale droplets of blood welled up.

There was nothing for it but, groaning, to get up again, wipe the wound with alcohol, bandage it, grab the .22 from behind the couch and open the door. The squirrel scurried onto the picnic table and Percy blew his head off, thus making Rocky the first casualty of Donna's engagement.

He kicked the body into the trees, and stood listening to the echoes of the rifle's report. The sound was startling in a state park where shooting was illegal—doubly so when a two-time felon forbidden guns pulled the trigger. But the echoes died out without rousing ranger sirens, and that was that.

That was that, except that, unusually for a weeknight, Percy cracked open a bottle of Kentucky Tavern. He missed Rocky's sympathetic ear and chattering counsel as he reviewed the history of Mark's worming his way into his family, but by the time

Letterman came on, Kentucky Tavern was running low and he could only nod and snore.

The next morning he woke up still in his chair to a dire, if relentlessly cheerful, Kansas City traffic report.

## 3.

PERCY WAS DRAGGING later as he cleaned cages. Much as on a Monday.

Sunday was his usual day for drowning such issues as being dependent for a living on the man who cuckolded him and seduced his daughter. Sundays Ranger Ray stood in for him at the ranger station and Percy *drank*.

He disappeared to his trailer Saturday evening, his six-day workweek completed, not to reappear until it was time to open up the ranger station Monday morning at 8:00 a.m. Until then he barricaded himself inside the Airstream—locked the door, closed the drapes, turned on the TV, ripped open a box of cookies and a bottle, and went to work.

Monday morning he would open up on time. Early, even; whatever the state of his head, he liked to give some time away. But on Mondays Percy carried himself with a dignity terrible to behold.

So too this Wednesday: He was moving with the majesty of a bishop.

After lunch, Maureen, a particular workamper friend of his, drove over to the ranger station to practice on the daunting new forms that Dennis decreed were to be filled out with every booth shift.

Or so she said. Percy took it as an invitation to drop by her trailer later. Well, maybe he would, if he felt like it.

"Congratulations, father-of-the-bride."

"You heard?"

"News travels," Maureen answered. "It's about time."

She floated some gift ideas, but his gruffness in response made her without further ado take a seat at Mark's desk in the back room; as usual, the head ranger was absent.

The engines of the Fort Horace Fire Department trundled with their police escort into the park as scheduled, and firemen took up positions around the massive hogback of Big Bone Hill, from the apple orchard on its eastern side planted before the Civil War to the wooded western base. They unwound their hoses, tested the wind and placed their accelerants, preparing to cremate the never-plowed height's dead goosegrass and bluestem much as the Osage Indians used to in their own springtime ritual.

When the start signal crackled over the radio Percy paid no mind, but Maureen stood up to peer out the side windows.

She saw smoke begin to rise from the far side of the hill. Soon orange tongues were darting into the air and licking together, merging into a frontier of flame that, in obedience to the wind, came over the hilltop as though to flee the billowing clouds of its own smoke. Fire defined the whole humped outline of Big Bone, and Maureen had trouble holding off the idea that it was coming for her. But at Apple Lane the waiting firemen washed the smoke white, revealing the hill behind wiped black with char.

It was, as always, vaguely disturbing. Smoke crawled over to envelop the ranger station, and a little seeped inside. It brought to mind Baghdad that week — shock and awe, TV screens blossoming with explosions in night-vision green.

Coughing, Maureen said, "Oh well, how would we ever know we lived in heaven without the *occasional* reminder of hell?"

No response. She sat down again and, having filled in another sample form, ran numbers on the calculator. The results made her sigh heavily.

"Look, Maureen!"

"Not now, Percy," she said, cupping her ears. "Trying to concentrate."

"Ralphie wants to say hi."

She only half heard, for a second wondered if he were unzipping—*Ralphie?*—when he pushed his fist in front of her face. At first she thought it held a gun, then saw that what wrapped his hand was a *snake*.

From the front room—reached in a leap—she commanded, "Put that thing away!"

"Aw, Maureen, be nice." Stroking the snake's upright head, Percy approached again. "Ralphie's the biggest captive king snake in Barber County."

"*Now*, Percy!" She bumped against the door. Bells jangled. "*Really!*"

He backed off. "He likes to get out, too," he grumbled. "Not right to keep them in cages."

"Don't let them *out*, do you?"

"Sometimes a guy's filling out a fishing license?" he answered, putting the snake back in its glass box. "And Ralphie slithers over to say hello. More gregarious than the others."

"Don't believe you. Pull something like that and Mark would show you the door."

"Welcome to any time, the *twit*," he said, clanging the cage closed.

Bravado, Maureen knew. Mark was all Percy had. If not Mark, who'd ever give him a job half as good as his crummy ranger-station one, $8 an hour plus truck and trailer? Mark had a slave for life.

Like a kid—a kid who knows he's trouble—Percy flipped his sheaf of ginger hair as Maureen returned to the desk.

"Know who's marrying Donna?" he asked, his craggy features softening.

"Um. *Mark*, I do sincerely hope?"

"No, but splicing 'em?"

"Who?"

"Travis. All set, already talked to him."

"*Our* Travis? Why, Percy, Travis is nothing but a mail-order minister!"

She regretted it the instant she said it, even before she saw how he took it, angling his face away while it filled with blood in a slow burn.

Sitting down again, she reflected that, however thoughtless, what she said was true: Travis, mute mower of campground and meadows, whose rare utterances thanked *Jaysus!* for lemonade, expressed gratitude to *The Lord!* for a sunny day, had recently earned a gold-bordered State license through an online course.

"Reverend Harrison might be available," she called. "Have you checked?"

"Silly me," Percy answered, "keeping it in our happy little park family."

"I just want the best for Donna."

"And I *don't*?" he thundered. "Shame of it is, Maureen, when the rest of us are standing up there on Big Bone and Donna marries Mark, *you* won't be there."

"Percy, I'm *sorry*—"

There was a click and a squeak.

"No, I won't have it," he called. "Fucking shame, too."

"Now, Percy—"

He reappeared, holding a mouse by the tail.

"You're officially *disinvited*," he told her, brown eyes flashing gold beneath beetled brows. "Nothing to be done about it."

"Don't do this, Percy." She got up and followed him to the front. "You're always cutting yourself off—"

Bells jangled, and a stranger stepped inside.

"Afternoon," he said.

## 4.

PERCY AND MAUREEN looked at him.

Maureen wondered what he was thinking as he looked back. Tall and thin, he had dusty-dry cheeks and hair somewhat long. At first she thought, mistakenly, that he was a good deal younger than her 53 or Percy's 46, maybe because like a youth he kept open the option of flight, standing on the balls of his feet.

The mouse squealed, asking what the holdup was, and Percy flicked it into the king snake's cage. It fled to the top of an artfully placed branch and stood tense and still, its white fur bathed with fluorescence.

The inevitable was in play. Ralphie, coiled at the bottom, lay equally still, or more still yet. Something happened too subtle for humans to perceive, and the mouse began scratching frantically at the glass. Moving ineffably over its own length, the serpent struck. The mouse screamed, but the slow-motion process of swallowing began even as the hind legs kicked—fast at first, then with envenomed languor.

Percy turned to the stranger with his most guileless expression.

"Help you, sir?"

"Thanks so much," said the man humorously, as shown by his lidded eyes and droll tone. "I can see it's a veritable Eden."

"Oh, you mean the mouse, sir?" Percy quizzed, playing along. "Snakes have to eat, too, and they don't eat anything dead. One of

Nature's little arrangements."

He leaned back and showed his teeth as another man might pat his holster.

"Cool," said the man.

He started to speak, but Percy said, "And we're all about Nature here, sir."

The man waited before saying, "Great."

"Do our best, sir," Percy said, adjusting his hair with another flip. Over time Maureen had come to realize its red, though it looked dyed, was actually faded from the unimaginable hue it once was. In the morning Percy dashed it flat with a comb, and after that whipped it into shape with snaps of his head.

"Is Dennis around?" asked the man. "He's expecting me. My name's Jack, here to work in the booth over the summer?"

"Maureen, what time does Dennis get home? Six o'clock?"

"Or a quarter to," she answered, putting out her hand. "I'm Maureen. I work booth, too, Wednesday and Thursday evenings."

Smiling, Jack shook her hand. "I'm all day Fridays."

"And this is Percy Bratcher," she said. "He runs the park, isn't that so, Percy?"

"Glad to meet you," said Jack, extending his hand again.

Ignoring it, Percy leaned back on his elbows and nodded out the window at the spruce old motorhome idling in the smoky parking lot. "That your rig?"

"Yeah."

"Got a camping permit?"

"No, I haven't."

"Need a permit."

"Later, Percy," Maureen urged. "Dennis will have one for him."

"I don't know," Percy said.

"Then ask Mark."

"Mark's not here, you know that."

"Well, then, let Dennis deal with it."

"What do I do till Dennis gets home?" Jack asked.

*"Wait,"* said Percy, savoring every particle of his authority. "But not in here."

"I'd set up, Jack, if I were you," Maureen suggested. "Campground's just a few hundred yards on. You can see it from here, on the left halfway to the lake?"

"Maureen, how do you know where Mark wants them?"

"'*Them?*'" asked Jack.

"Him and his wife," Percy said as if Jack weren't there.

"I don't have a wife."

"No *wife?*" Percy asked. "Why *not?*"

"Percy!" said Maureen.

"Because I'm gay," said Jack. "Against the law for me to marry."

"Got *that* right," Percy said.

"Site 83's empty," Maureen told Jack rapidly. "Right next to mine. Good gravel *and* a sewer connection. Follow me, I'll show you. Percy, he can set up, if Mark doesn't like it, he can move later on."

"Fuck. Get him a thingy for the pole."

"In here, Jack," she said, and he followed her into Mark's office while she looked for a plasticine orange *V* that, slipped into the utility stalk, signalized a volunteer's site. Quietly she said, "Don't mind Percy, his bark's worse than his bite. You'll like it here, and we're glad to have you."

"Thanks," said Jack, taking in the posters on the walls. Most showed wildflowers, but an old one captioned *Ski Kansas* depicted a skier crouched in a wheat field's snowy stubble.

Maureen found what she was looking for and turned to leave, but Jack recoiled.

"What's *that?*" He pointed at something hanging, aimed at the customers, in the darkness beneath the counter.

Percy came alive.

"*This* ol' thing?" Stepping up, he stooped, inevitably groaning, and with a sweep of his arm lifted it into the light. It looked quaint, like a pirate's matchlock pistol. "Never seen a sawed-off shotgun before?"

"Don't know that I have."

"Best little problem-solver going," Percy assured him, cradling it. "'Case things get out of hand."

He swung it out, not exactly aiming at Jack, and racked it: Ker-*chunkt!*

Every inch of Maureen's bowel spasmed. Percy stood there smiling his smile that was like a snarl.

"*Cool*," said Jack.

"Let's go find your site, Jack," Maureen said.

"Appreciate it, Maureen," he said cheerily. "Thanks, Percy."

"Any time, *sir!*"

As Jack held the door for her, Maureen heard Percy breathe, "*Faggot.*" Then, out loud, "OK, guys, who's hungry?"

## 5.

JACK FOLLOWED MAUREEN'S Durango to the campground, found Site 83 next door to her yellow travel trailer and backed into it—ably, if he said so himself. He reversed the captain's chairs, pulled the curtains, attached the water and sewer hoses, plugged in the electric and slipped the *V* into the stalk.

"Well, girl, can't say I care for the jerk in the ranger station," he reported to Lady as he clambered back inside, "but we shouldn't have much to do with him, and otherwise I think we'll like it here.

Hope so, anyway."

His site, like the others, had a picnic table and raised grill, a swath of turf and a tree—a silver maple, just beginning to bud. Laid out around pretzels of asphalt looping beneath Big Bone Hill, the campground covered more than 100 acres and was surrounded by woods. It offered no view of the lake. Dotting it were two or three dozen tumbledown rigs of residents, as well as the trimmer rigs of volunteers and a few overnight visitors.

Because volunteers could stay indefinitely at whatever site they chose—whereas residents had to "hop" to a new one every two weeks—their rigs were concentrated towards the western side, where the woods assured a wedge of shade creeping eastward on summer afternoons, when shade was a prized commodity, and staked with claims to permanence: bird feeders, bird baths, skirting that hid wheels, fanciful signs emblazoned with fanciful names. So permanent were the satellite dishes lashed to them that vines spiraled up their legs.

For the rest of the day Jack walked Lady, tracing the loops, following the road to the marina and boat ramps, and wandering the network of paths in the woods bordering the lake. Later, Big Bone Hill steaming wispily, he decided to climb it. Immediately they encountered Maureen, just returning from a walk with Maggie, her golden retriever.

The dogs, after sniffing each other, went down on their front paws, offering to play.

"Well, *friends*," said Maureen.

"And did I see a cat in your window?" Jack asked.

"Two cats."

"A wealth of them, then."

Maureen asked Jack about himself.

"Just healing," he told her, "or trying to, like I guess the whole country. My partner died, and after 9/11 I lost my job, finally moved into my rig, spent the winter in Texas, and here I am!"

# THE WEDDING ON BIG BONE HILL

Nodding understandingly, she disclosed that she was widowed, too, while Jack thought how Cameron's death was old news by now. But obviously something had frozen up, though he wasn't sure what, and he'd been staring into space across the Southwest with a pleasant feeling of decompression.

With a "See you later!" he and Lady headed up Big Bone. Near its base were fenceposts topped by flat, fierce-looking skulls. The skulls that gave it its name, Maureen later told him, came from the possums that proverbially converge on it to die.

The hill was volcanically black, save for a serpentine turf pathway spared by design whose fresh green stood out against the char like a hieroglyph. A brisk climb up its couple hundred feet and Jack was breathing hard.

The views went far past the gray lake to farmland rolling to every horizon save the eastern one, where the town of Fort Horace sprouted steeples over buildings of brick and stone. The sun was setting on a grand scale. Jack could see three distinct weather systems—to the south a scrim of showers, to the west castleworks of clouds rearing up, and in the north a band of black cracked by lightning. East of the Missouri River the sky's a local affair, but in the West it becomes the immense, the epic, the planetary sky.

He saw a little blue truck pull up to the trailer Maureen had pointed out as Dennis's, near the ranger station and directly across from the closed-up entrance booth.

"C'mon, girl, let's go meet the boss."

They descended the path and walked up the road, Lady pulling eagerly past the ranger station, dark except for a Coke machine winking from the porch.

In a window of the trailer Jack saw a man draining a can of beer. He knocked and the man opened the door, bending outside like a big-headed figure peering from a fairy-tale cottage.

"Hi, I'm Jack. Are you Dennis?"

"*Yes!*" said Dennis. "Come on in. Sure, her too."

Dennis found a dog biscuit for Lady and an Old Milwaukee for Jack, and sat them down in his neat, nicotine-tallowed living room. Its minute scale made Jack feel eight feet tall. Dennis was a pudgy, eagerly smiling 35 or so. Empty beer cans ringed his chair. As they talked Jack was aware of a furtive scrutiny of his face and crotch, and had a sense of disappointment.

After asking about his trip and what he thought of the park, Dennis explained what the job working booth involved.

Although Big Bone was a state park, visitors had to pay admission, and Jack, selling permits at the booth, would be working as Dennis's agent. Recent legislation privatized the sale of state-park permits, handing the job over to a bonded Vendor for each park—for Big Bone, *him!* From each sale, whether of a $50 annual pass or a $5 daily, Dennis would pocket $1.

Jack formally accepted the job, and Dennis gave him an array of permit books, a sheaf of forms and a starting bank of $100 in silver and small bills, getting his receipt in return. After going over the ins and outs of the different permits and forms, he also gave him a camping permit, assuring him Mark would approve his selection of Site 83.

Dennis further explained that he would himself share Saturday/Sunday duties with the couple he'd finally succeeded in recruiting. He daily expected the Beanblossoms to show up in their designated site across the lawn from his trailer.

Nervously, he let drop that he'd been expecting the Beanblossoms for weeks. After advertising all winter added no one to his inherited roster—Maureen was to work her third season of Wednesday/Thursday half-shifts, while Monday/Tuesday would again be taken by Rupert, a taciturn retired farmer—Dennis had promptly accepted the Beanblossoms when they volunteered.

Ever since, as the season approached, Sherry Beanblossom had been sending emoticon-spangled emails chronicling delays— repairs, her kid's earache and her own "attack :-( :-( :-(." But that very day she'd announced their arrival in Chanute, not far to the south, "enjoying the FREE :-) :-) :-) city campground while we replace a fuse. LOL!!!"

Having refused a third beer, Jack took his leave. As he walked home rain clouds were besieging the park. In the dying light, the streetlights popping on at each loop's showerhouse emphasized the campground's emptiness, which he thought resembled a cemetery studded with fiberglass mausoleums.

The first cold drops were striking when they reached the rig. Indoors, Jack fed Lady, found some cold chicken for himself, then, rain pattering on the roof, regarded the cozy interior of their home as he ate.

It was an ochre-colored 1969 Cortez motorhome, a handsome, glassy confection he'd picked up cheap on eBay, confident outside, inside retaining snug, dated glamour. It was a relic of an optimistic period; the Apollo astronauts traveled to the launch pad aboard a NASA Cortez. It had couches, a kitchen, dining booth, double bed, double bunk and bathroom. Jack had replaced the original carpeting with new stuff in the same style: green shag. Surfaces were either avocado-colored enamel or paneled in wood.

That interior had housed him all over the Southwest; wherever he went, he found himself in the same place. Then again, against his expectations and even his hopes, he was finding out how the self can travel through different scenes untouched by them, how travel in fact *heightens* the sense of self. Making every trip an ego trip.

Still, he was healing. The drumbeat of rain on the roof had to be helping.

## 6.

LATE THAT EVENING, in streaming hat and mackintosh, Percy made one of his flashlight foot patrols of the campground. His eagle eye was ever on the lookout for infractions of park rules. His conviction was that everybody tries to get away with *something*, but that anyone allowed to get away with *anything* will try to get away with *more*, and he (if he alone) could see where *that* leads.

He being the poster child for getting away with *nothing*.

Hence his interest in leaks or loose fittings, expired permits, sites with cars parked on the grass or more vehicles than permits, in noise, litter, fires set outside the grills, strewn toys, bones, dog droppings—anything he could see as he crouched beside a rig (painfully suppressing his groan) or crawled underneath it. Anything that might justify a late-night knock on the door.

If a generator intruded on "quiet hours," Percy raised holy hell, bawling out the malefactor in a voice that carried across the campground. The same if he sniffed the marijuana popular with a certain element, or found anyone drinking liquor in the open air— an activity as popular as it was forbidden. He was particularly vigilant against sex atop the picnic tables, a lamentably common summertime infraction.

And if he found an American flag abandoned to the darkness, without the spotlight the law decrees be trained on it, Percy didn't care *how* late it was, he banged on the door and made whoever answered fix the problem or face immediate expulsion.

Cautiously, he approached Jack's rig and played his beam over it. From Maureen's trailer next door came the ebb and flow of television, her windchimes tinkling as raindrops plashed them. The Cortez was quiet, though when he was within a few feet of it he heard music he couldn't quite make out.

He squatted, training the light beneath the chassis. No trash. No droppings. No leaks from the sewer hose, no faint hiss from the propane tank—in fact, despite the rig's age, no tank at all, but modern bottles fitted with safety valves. Nothing out of order.

No one in his *life* had ever *volunteered* to him he was *gay*. Proclaimed it. *Boasted*. Had it been, as in retrospect he suspected, an *advance*? At the very thought, Percy's skin shivered, his nostrils curled, his gut rocked. Not since his standoff with Mark had he encountered anyone who so incited his whole being.

The music finally registered as classical, which made him snort, and that set the dog to barking, to the point that the door swung open to Jack gripping Lady's collar.

Hearing, "See, girl? No one there," Percy rose up groaning into the light.

Exploding in snarls, Lady dragged Jack halfway through the door before he managed to stuff her indoors and step outside. Percy didn't move.

"Evening," said Jack.

"What's going on?" Percy asked.

"Scared my dog."

"I mean what else?"

"You tell *me* what's going on."

"Don't get your back up, just saying hi."

Jack was silent.

"Nice rig. Collector's item?"

"King of the road in its day," agreed Jack, ignoring the other's sneer.

"No satellite dish?"

"Nah."

"Well, we get CBS pretty good. Sometimes Fox."

"Great."

"Barking's against the rules, by the way."

"You *made* her bark."

"Happen again, have to get rid of her. Just so you know."

"Terrific. Thanks."

"Any time."

Percy walked on. Jack watched him circle the loop, putting his flashlight to rigs on either side, once banging on a door to lambaste someone about something.

## 7.

IT RAINED UNTIL DAWN.

Jack stirred as residents' noisy trucks fired up to take them to their jobs landscaping or on local farms or at the nearby box factory, but he rolled over and slept again until fully 10:00 a.m., when he tumbled into clothes fit for public view and walked Lady around the loop. Then he fed her and enjoyed an hour drinking coffee in the chilly sun.

After breakfast and his first, lukewarm shower at the nearest showerhouse, he strapped a pack to his shoulders and pedaled off on his old Trek to explore the town and find some groceries.

Riding past Big Bone and out of the park, he coasted downhill on a biking/walking path (Fort Horace prided itself on being bicycle-friendly). He passed woods—a bobcat slipped into a culvert at his approach—farms, housing tracts, a shopping center, a branch of the state college. Arriving downtown, he hitched his bike to a rack.

In the drive up from Texas Jack had made about Kansas the discovery that can be made about any state: It is a veritable kingdom unto itself, with a fervent life of its own unsuspected by outsiders. As usual staying off the Interstate, he'd passed through dozens of towns that dramatized the prairie thrill at human community, storefronts jammed companionably together beneath towering grain elevators, houses crowding near as they could.

Walking Fort Horace's streets, he was taken with the town's handsome look and long-settled air, and admired the old mercantile fronts, fine churches, solid office blocks, the warehouses along the river. Stepping into the Carnegie library with its glassy addition, he browsed its well-chosen collection, pleased to learn that a postmarked envelope addressed to him at the park would enable him to get a library card.

Also he spent a rewarding hour visiting the town's namesake fort. Built in the 1840s, Fort Horace made one of that irregular line of cavalry forts—Fort Kearny, Fort Scott, Fort Washita, Fort Smith, among many others—that long held that borderline of the id, the frontier between settled America and the menacing, beckoning Indian lands beyond. Around a parade ground rose brick barracks, stables, and a gunpowder magazine in proportions as graceful as they were four-square; two dignified rows of officers' houses overlooked the river. Even as it made its statement of force, Fort Horace proclaimed a high and confident opinion of the young republic it served.

Afterwards, seeing turrets rise over bare branches, Jack gasped uphill to discover a street parallel to Main but removed to the upper atmosphere that better suits money. Triumphant mansions of a later generation lined it, improving upon the fort's architecture with Victorian furbelows.

Before leaving town Jack shopped at the Hy-Vee store, then climbed back on his bike and pointed himself at Big Bone Hill, which loomed up to block the sun. As he pedaled—*and* pedaled, *and* pedaled—its unchanging bulk fixed him in an immensity of space, three dimensions defined by duration, the fourth.

To experience thus the intransigence of the Western landscape replicates a sliver of the experience of the pioneers crossing it, their progress mocked by implacably distant landmarks.

It was, Jack thought, kind of great.

## 8.

AS JACK CAME PANTING up, Maureen and Maggie were walking into Picnic Park Way.

The Picnic Park, Fort Horace's outlying (and free) municipal picnic grounds, abutted the state park. A hundred yards short of the booth stood a stone statue of an Osage chieftain, weathered almost to the skeleton, and there Picnic Park Way branched off in a mile-long circle through woods overlooking the lake.

"Hi, Jack. Out and about already?"

"Yes, got to town!"

He turned and kept pace with her, talking about what he'd seen. When he exclaimed at the hill of grand Victorians, Maureen told him how she used to live in one of them. He exclaimed again as they came to a stone-and-timber pavilion with a dramatic roofline; she explained that it, along with a dozen others farther along, was a legacy of the WPA.

Jack soon said goodbye and rode on ahead.

The sun had been out all day, but with little effect on the air's rawness. Even so, Maureen sensed an impending awakening. She supposed she was ready, but she did love winter and the isolation it imposed. Snow could keep her in her camper a week at a time, content to be enshrouded by a blanket of white, pristine but for the tracks of deer and Maggie's yellow contributions near the door, while the fierce hot breath of the propane furnace fought the cold.

# THE WEDDING ON BIG BONE HILL

Her affair with Percy Bratcher ("If I have to call it that," she told herself) began the day two years earlier when, a widow of six month's standing, she hauled her trailer into the park. For a decade she and her husband vacationed in it at a lake in Missouri, but in all that time Maureen had never towed it, so the sensation of having her tail plucked as she drove down the road was a novel one.

She stopped at the ranger station to buy a camping permit. Percy filling it out at the counter reminded her of a Western movie hero; his rugged face yet bore the improbable imprint of early prettiness. She watched him until she realized *he* was watching *her*. Her spine thrilled, but she just thanked him and went on, chose a site and was having an impossible time backing into it when Percy drove up, dismounted, walked over—legs giving wide berth to whatever hung between—and took over.

Once they had her trailer plugged in, she invited him inside for coffee. But they both knew what she meant.

Apparently, she reflected, she was one of those widows free to act frankly for the first time in her life—to do what she wanted with the pent-up desire of a long marriage. Not the way she was raised, nor the way she lived 29 years with Stan, but as she got older she was learning to make a life out of what lies at hand.

As one must; Nature leaves off, uninterested, after the courtship years, and life's remainder has to be improvised, for Nature has nothing to command, except to die. There were not lacking those to tell her how weird and irresponsible it was to sell the house and move into the camper. They shut up long ago about not having kids, which she supposed was simply recognition of her age. So Percy seemed a gift.

He suited her, wielding his manhood like a battering ram, without finesse. It was not finesse Maureen wanted. Abetting him in finding fugitive freedom between her legs was, for her, a kind of self-gratification. With the guilty bonus of not having him around the house to feed or clean up after or endure.

Percy even got her the job working booth, announcing to old Mrs. Godwin, the park employee who then ran it, that Maureen would handle Wednesday and Thursday evenings from then on. It beat paying site rent or hopping every two weeks, and gave her, in season, just enough to do.

She loved not him, never *Percy*, but the adult matter-of-factness and freedom they acted on. If she wanted to get together with him, she might stop by the ranger station and pick up her mail. Conversely, he might bring a letter by after work. In warm weather they'd sit outside, enjoying a drink from coffee mugs — his bourbon, hers the Chablis she bought by the box — and waving to passers-by, until they transferred indoors, where what they did so briskly made her grateful her trailer possessed sufficient mass to resist the bouncing small ones (or worse, tent-trailers!) can get themselves into.

Their trysts ended abruptly. A mighty grunt signaled Percy's final thrust and their mutual collapse into a silence on her side contented, though she was often curious why he had nothing to say, nothing to offer, until he withdrew and wiped himself on her floral sheets.

A shyness that endeared him to her descended as he visibly wanted *out* but felt awkward about it. For maybe two seconds. Then he swung over and pulled on his clothes, patted her on the head or rump, and saw himself out. Whistling as soon as he closed the door behind him, like a man coming out of a public restroom after a good shit.

Only a very few times did he instead fall asleep. On those occasions his groans gave way to a baby's placid breathing. She would scour that weathered face of his, younger than hers, but pitted with so much more of life's bombardment, his mouth for once slack and open, drool collecting at its lower edge. The least touch then and he seized awake, eyes wide, body jackknifing. The *least* touch; the merest fingertip brushing a meaty shoulder called forth the same exaggerated response—even a stray caress of that shank of hair that preserved a reminder of the flames that licked about his head when he was young.

Once he slept an hour. Ever so gradually his body relaxed and settled into hers, his head unconcernedly softening her breasts for his pillow, making their two bodies one compatible mass, until some unconscious crossing of intimacy's boundary, or some memory poking out of its shroud, sounded an alarm, his body bunched away and his eyes snapped open in fear that instantly slid into the sneer he would give a whore.

They never went anywhere. Never much talked. If Maureen had a flat tire, it wasn't Percy she called. If Donna needed motherly advice, it wasn't Maureen her father turned to (in fact, Maureen felt their *thing* was a bar to her getting to know Donna). But it was a workable arrangement, and if it gave rise to comment, that discomfited neither.

At first it surprised her that she didn't want to be closer to him. But she came to realize that what Percy touched to her was the outer edge of a vast and scary unhappiness. She declined to try assuaging it; his problems were too terrifically out of proportion to her own. As he performed with her his losing fight for freedom, she took what she needed and left it at that.

Whether that unhappiness was owing to his time in prison, or prison owing to his unhappiness, she didn't presume to guess. Like everyone in the park, she knew about the standoff and the shooting. She also knew that nobody got hurt either time, except Percy.

By disinviting her to Donna's wedding, tacitly characterizing their relationship as something stuck to his shoe he'd finally kicked free of, Percy was consigning her to virtually a second widowhood. Pity for them both washed over her, especially as, following Maggie through the Picnic Park, she saw a sure sign of spring.

Two empty cars were parked at the pavilion whose walls bore

the names of WPA grandees. It was known as the gazebo, and people whispered about what men did under its roof. Low voices made Maggie prick up her ears. Cold for love in the open air, Maureen thought, pulling her dog onwards before anyone could come out and have to glaze a sex-softened expression at sight of them.

Maggie was doing her business near the next pavilion when the men returned to their cars, one moving with loose-limbed youth, the other more heavily. The elder pulled out without appearing to see Maureen. The younger waved as he drove past.

They weren't the only ones, it turned out. At the last pavilion a truck and empty car were parked side by side. A man sat in the truck, apparently alone, until a woman's head bobbed up beside his. Immediately it sank again. The man's eyes followed Maureen in his mirror.

Picnic Park Way carried her and Maggie back to the road, where beneath the gaze of the Osage chief they stepped from the trees into open country that held the sweep of the West. The park road in fact followed the Oregon Trail right up to where the lake drowned it at the boat ramps; ruts 170 years old were preserved near Apple Lane. From the parting of low hills to the north she could hear the scream of the Interstate.

Percy drove up, probably headed out to the Hy-Vee. She waved him to a stop.

"How's-it?" he asked pleasantly.

"Percy, I *am* sorry for my mail-order-minister crack," she said. "Travis will be *perfect*."

Of itself, Percy's truck pulled six inches forward.

"Thinking about this Jack character," he said. "Worried, you get my drift. State park, little boys in here every day? Overnight?"

"*Dennis* is—"

A half-foot more. "There's no harm in Dennis. But *this* guy. Never know what they're up to. Or pardon me, that's just the problem: You *do*."

"Oh, Percy, he seems very nice."

"I mean, if *that's* a man, what am *I*?" His truck stole far enough forward that to hold her gaze with eyes glaring amber Percy had to turn his head. "He's got *something* going on. Lives in an RV for a reason."

"Don't we all?" she asked.

But she was talking to his taillights.

## 9.

MAUREEN INAUGURATED the season a few days later, unlocking the booth Wednesday afternoon at 4:00 o'clock, an hour before Percy closed up the ranger station. Jack accompanied her so he could learn the ropes.

The booth stood in the middle of the entry lanes. Like all the park structures, it had a steep shake roof that made it resemble a miniature Pizza Hut. Inside there was room for two to man the sliding windows, though two-person crews were resorted to only on the long Memorial Day, Fourth of July and Labor Day weekends. Just past the booth was a cut-through to the exit lane, for use by the sizable proportion of visitors who, declining to pay, preferred instead to turn around and take their recreation for free in the Picnic Park.

Inside, everything was as it had been left at the close of the previous season, Pompeii-like, save for the sprinkling of dead flies on the window sills. As with any workplace, the booth had its own peculiar weather. Its counter was littered with long-expired permits, someone's lost driver's license, a paperback romance, pizza menus, stray batteries, ballpoints, paperclips, rubber bands eaten at by the sun.

"Nice," said Jack.

"Nice," Maureen agreed. Hanging up a bag of dog biscuits—every visiting dog got one—she spread her permit books over the counter, set up her bank and took one of the tall chairs. April traffic would mostly consist of residents coming home from work, their vehicles pausing until she saw the permit on the windshield and released them with a wave.

She asked Jack whether Dennis had set him up with permits and a bank.

"Gave me everything I needed," Jack assured her, "including two beers in ten minutes."

"Dennis does like his beer," she said.

"You think?" Jack replied. Dennis had told him he drank an 18-pack every night, but Jack didn't get the idea he *liked* beer. More that he had a job to do and did it—soldiered on to that last can whether he wanted to or not.

Maureen turned on the air conditioner for a minute to make sure it worked, tapped the weather radio (getting the forecast), and pushed a button on the shortwave, placing the booth in contact with the park network—ranger station, ranger trucks, Percy's truck and trailer, some volunteers' rigs. It would chatter intermittently, unobtrusively all day long. Mark had recently supplemented the shortwave with walkie-talkie cellphones for himself, the rangers and Percy.

She also pulled Percy's laminated signs off the windows. "Maximum three per tent aloud" was her favorite, but there were also the warring "Pay at ranger station when booth closed" and "When booth closed pay at self-pay kiosk."

Jack asked about another:

> **NO KITES**
> ***NONE!***

She told him the story behind it: One day a motorhome pulled into the ranger station. Its driver wouldn't have stood out in a crowd, save perhaps by virtue of his jaunty yachtsman's cap. Percy, impatiently filling out a camping permit, asked his rig's make.

The man responded quietly, but with due force, "It's a Prevost." He pronounced it with classy faux Frenchiness: "Pre-*voh*." Prevosts cost more than a million dollars apiece.

That was the end of Percy's resistance to giving him the 50-amp site he wanted; he canceled someone else's reservation.

But the next day, a windy one, the man was back in his tow vehicle (which Percy noted approvingly was a Hummer), trembling and white-faced: In the campground two kids of eight or ten had been flying a bright red kite, and naturally while it was soaring over the Pre-*voh* the wind died, the kite heeled over and dived onto its roof. Dived onto the roof of the Pre-*voh* and *dented* it.

Percy ascertained the shocking fact by closing up the ranger station, driving over and hoisting himself, groaning, up the Pre-*voh*'s rear ladder. There was indeed a small depression; moreover, the paint was scratched. He apologized abjectly and promised to run the miscreants out of the park. And did so: He found the boys—not at all surprised to learn they belonged to a tent-trailer—and expelled them and their parents.

"So that's why 'No Kites,'" Maureen concluded.

"Wasn't it the Taliban that banned kites?" Jack murmured. "Makes you wonder why Mark gives Percy so much power."

"Percy's very efficient," Maureen said, sharply for her. "Give it to Percy to do and it's *done*. He's smart and a self-starter. If he didn't have a record, he'd go a long way."

"Suicidal, if you carry it forward."

"What do you mean by *that*?"

"Well, when someone like Mark doesn't do his job," Jack said, "the vacuum will less often be filled by your smart self-starters than by your righteous punishers—someone who'll placate a rich guy by forbidding kids to play. But I guess if you live in hell, you want to pull everyone else in with you."

"You're too apocalyptic, Jack," Maureen said stiffly.

A trickle of cars gave him practice with actual customers—he greeted them with a bright "Welcome!"—and Maureen introduced him to residents coming home from their jobs. Some fellow volunteers also passed. Most were retired house-proud couples, many ex-military, who seemed outgoing and wary in equal measure.

Jack had already met one family along his loop: Chuck was a retired libertarian Kansas City printer of wit and conviction. He and his wife, Charlene, cared for their grandson, who in contradistinction to his grandparents was African-American. Brendan was 15 and had an athletic figure to go with his friendly, lonely smile. Jack suspected he was gay, so was already keeping his distance.

When a Corvette paused in the far lane, Maureen called, "Hi, Mark!"

"Hey, Gorgeous," responded the dark, compact person behind the wheel. He had a mustache and the hollow cheeks and preoccupied expression of a man harrowed by hormones.

"Just showing Jack."

"Hey, Jack," said Mark, driving on.

"What did Percy *do*, anyway?" Jack asked.

And Maureen told him that, too.

## 10.

MARK'S DEPREDATIONS were legendary long before Percy hauled his little green trailer, wife and two kids into the park (Mark's father being who he was—a former governor—no change in behavior was anticipated).

Out of season, the park's daytime population was tiny: Mark plus three rangers, the salaried maintenance staff of four the State deemed sufficient to keep up 5,000 acres, and a dozen stay-at-home wives in trailers and motorhomes. Most female residents worked outside the park, but some lived in a kind of purdah inside their RVs, kept company by *Oprah*, seldom stepping out of their rigs when their menfolk were away.

Whatever the attraction they held for him, Mark felt compelled to try to seduce them all. And duly found left-behind wives susceptible to the fascination of the man with the powers of site selection, of providing extra amperage or overlooking excessive water use.

If Mark also plowed the field of visitors, many of them, after all, came to the park to party. He kept tabs through bicycle patrols through the campground, riding his Cannondale in his tailored ranger's shirt and shorts.

At the time Percy worked as a silo cleaner. Grain can rathole a silo—that is, build up around the edges, reducing its capacity. Someone had to shovel up the moldering stuff, and do it without causing an explosion. For, unlikely as it may seem, an atmosphere of corn or wheat particles charged with static electricity is but a spark away from fueling a bomb that can level a town.

Hence Percy, masked and naked, or nearly so, his hair sometimes standing on end, wielded the wooden shovels and pails of his trade so as to forestall the blast. It was hard work but comparatively lucrative and year-round, as not all jobs in farm country are, and since in rapid succession he'd been thrown out of high school and the Army for fighting (which last he insisted was the irony of ironies), it was the best he could do.

Mark seduced Percy's wife. It wasn't much of a challenge; Pam was deadly bored. She arranged for a neighbor lady to watch the kids during their assignations. One day an approaching thunderstorm sent Percy home early, by way of a tavern; silos can't be cleaned with lightning in the vicinity. Finding the neighbor lady in his trailer, he asked where his wife was. When she finally told him, Percy grabbed his deer rifle and drove up to Mark's house, perched among trees on the rise behind the ranger station.

The ranger was just loading Pam into his vintage cherry-red Corvette when Percy burst out of his truck and trained his rifle on him. Mark was unarmed. Percy walked up and prodded his face with the barrel. Mark angled his head back, but otherwise didn't move. Pam screamed for a few minutes, then drove off in Percy's smoking old Ram, hardly daring to peep over the steering wheel.

The two men stood there, Percy poking at the other's head and neck, Mark fighting to keep his balance. Meanwhile, in one of Nature's easy theatrical touches, the threatened thunderstorm blew in and roared and flashed around them, soaking them and making it seem silly to stand there. But they stood unmoving even after it passed, Percy sighting along the barrel to Mark's head, not meeting his eyes, which were unfocussed anyway, but not pulling the trigger, either.

It was extraordinary, but he couldn't summon the necessary smidgeon of muscular strength to do it.

When the cops roared up—aiming guns and shouting at the top of their lungs—Percy shut his eyes and, to his everlasting shame, lowered his rifle.

For the first time in his life he let down the code he lived by, choosing life over manhood; one little lapse, but enough to eat him up forever.

Should have blown the motherfucker's head off, he admitted it.

He tried to keep his wife's infidelity out of his trial, for pride's sake and the children's. Blaming liquor alone, he got no sympathy from judge or jury. Sentenced to five years, he served three.

As for Mark, the standoff polished his legend—until Percy burnished it even brighter.

For, six months after he was released from prison to his old job and empty trailer (everyone thought it stupefyingly gracious of Mark even to allow him back in the *park*), one evening Percy, drunk and determined to make up for his earlier lapse, though now an ex-con barred from owning guns, borrowed another resident's antique Enfield rifle, climbed the slope behind the ranger station and shot at Mark repeatedly (and quite harmlessly) through his living room windows. The Enfield's distinctive shell casings gave him away immediately.

After serving five full years, Percy came out again and couldn't find a job—a new acoustic device made his silo-cleaning skills obsolete. With positively lordly forbearance Mark offered him a job doing ranger-station scutwork, and Percy had to take it. He had no choice if he wanted custody of his daughter, even if it meant that Mark carried his balls in his pocket forevermore. They were locked in a dance, Percy the bear on a chain, Mark from a safe distance taunting: *Who's got the balls now?*

"Wow," said Jack when Maureen finished. It was dark.

"Well, this part of the state has a tragic dimension from way back, anyway."

"Oh?"

"Oh Lord, in Civil War times? Right here on Apple Lane, a mob lynched an abolitionist. Over in Osawatomie, John Brown shelled pro-slavery houses. And in Lawrence? Quantrill's Confederate raiders massacred more than 200 men and boys."

"Jesus."

"And at the Statehouse? The man who shot John Wilkes Booth

was doorkeeper—*before* he vanished, but *after* he castrated himself. Fact."

When Dennis drove in and learned that Maureen hadn't sold a permit for an hour, he suggested she close down for the night.

Scooping up her bank and permit books, she assured Jack, "Really it's a lot of fun. You'll enjoy it."

# 11.

JACK'S OWN FIRST SHIFT—his noon-to-9:00 Friday marathon—came two days later. He hurried to the booth, arriving with Fort Horace's noontime whistle, breathlessly slapped down his permits, organized his bank and looked up at the empty road curving past the Osage chief down into the trees, the sky beyond piling itself high over the shoulders of the Great Plains.

The road stayed empty for an hour. Finally a car nosed around the curve and made its way towards him. Despite sudden stage fright, Jack came out with "Welcome!" and completed his first transaction, collecting $5 for a daily pass, scrawling the date on it in Magic Marker and pressing its glue end to the car's windshield.

The day took on a rhythm. There wasn't much to do, but neither was it boring. It couldn't be, not with the booth's windows organizing a landscape of continental amplitude.

As he was beginning to look out for Dennis's coming home and spelling him for dinner, a streamlined land yacht rounded the curve and cleared the trees. It was an opulent old beast, a blue-and-silver empress of the highways coming on with a panache unknown to our boxier age. Its headlights, futuristically shielded by fogged Plexiglas, swam forward in the dusk like an aged beauty's watery eyes. Mismatched beads of lights defined the roofline behind swooping chrome trumpets that, as she neared the booth, blatted raspberries.

"Fuck, I don't know why," the driver was saying when he unjammed his sliding window. "Sounded good earlier."

"Fart it again, Ernie," an unseen boy urged.

"Shut the fuck up, you little bugger," said the driver, even as he fought off the Rottweiler that romped across his lap to shove its head out snarling. Beneath a faded wife-beater he had the frame of one for generations underfed, his hair straggly and mustache scraggly. The length of his straw-colored hair hid neither its thinness nor his hairline's deep recession.

From the shadows enveloping the other captain's chair a woman's voice as high and cultivated as Eleanor Roosevelt's cried out, "Greetings! You see Sherry and Ernie Beanblossom arriving at last!"

"Welcome," Jack managed to say. "We've been expecting you. Here's your site right here." He pointed to the gravel drive at the edge of Dennis's lawn.

"Thank you!"

The motorhome pulled past the booth, revealing hooded taillights and a Continental kit with cursive chrome lettering, plus a flatbed trailer holding an old Chevy Astro minivan. Ernie got out, slanted planks behind and backed the van off. Unhitching the trailer with the help of the boy, a plump twelve-year-old named Bobby, he pushed it onto the lawn and backed the van up to it.

Perching again on his captain's chair — Jack was surprised he could reach the pedals — he backed into the site with one deft turn of the wheel, then got out and shambled over to the booth.

"Mission accomplished," he said.

"Elegant rig," said Jack.

"Top of the line," Ernie declared.

The woman was left leaning on a wheelchair with an oxygen tank on its seat, pushing it slowly but determinedly towards the booth. Her muumuu did not disguise her enormousness. Three hundred pounds looked sure, 350 not out of the question.

"Hope your wife's all right."

"ERNIE! DO IT OVER."

"Got her breath, anyway," Ernie muttered. Turning around, he whined, "Fuck's wrong, Sherry?"

"LEAVE MORE GRAVEL ON THIS SIDE SO WE DON'T STEP IN MUD LIKE IN SHREVEPORT."

Ernie obeyed. He jerked the craft onto the roadway and backed it in again, leaving a wider margin of gravel on the entry side.

"Satisfied?" he yelled.

"I'm hungry, Ma," said the boy.

"ERNIE!"

Dennis looked relieved when he drove in just then and saw the new arrivals, but as Sherry gasped her way past his headlights his expression turned to horror. "Oh my God," Jack heard him say softly.

Sherry reached the booth.

"Hello, I'm Sherry," she announced, Eleanor Roosevelt redux. "So pleased to meet you."

After introducing himself, Dennis expressed concern for her health.

"I *think* I'm all right," Sherry panted, "but in case of an attack I thought I'd better have my chair and oxygen handy. Fibromyalgia's like that. Some days to look at me you wouldn't think there was a thing in the world wrong, other days you'll find me planted in my wheelchair on oxygen."

"Hard to work booth in that condition," Dennis suggested.

"Jesus will see me through," Sherry replied. "And there's always Ernie."

Who tumbled against Dennis's truck just then, lunging for

Bobby's football pass. With the boy's help he resumed unloading onto the lawn a number of items that must have impeded passage inside the motorhome.

After Jack's dinner hour, Dennis, relieved in turn, ignited logs within a circle of rocks — his was the only fire ring in the park — and ducked indoors. As he emerged with chips, beer and a box of Chablis, flames were burning high and bright.

He offered the Beanblossoms beer. Ernie accepted after emphasizing how seldom he drank, Sherry only after making it clear that she never *drank* at all, but out of affectionate memory of her grandfather's giving her her first sips would accept a thimbleful. Soon, summoned via shortwave, Maureen and Maggie joined them.

Thus began Dennis's hospitable routine of nightly campfires.

Meanwhile Bobby strung Christmas lights from roof to earth at either end of the motorhome, as though it were a vessel at port in Cannes or Newport Beach. RV'ers love to proclaim the festive nature of their lives.

"Beauty, ain't it?" Sherry declared. "Bought it out of Ernie's settlement."

"Set us back $22,000," Ernie put in, pushing out his upper plate for the kicker: "*Cash!*"

"Settlement?" asked Maureen.

"My back," Ernie explained. "Working construction in Pennsylvania two years ago? I'm moving bricks, and *Holy* Mother of *God!* Torn in half, feels like. Cripple over, sit down. 'Off your ass, Beanblossom,' my foreman yells. 'Back's out,' I says. 'Just hurt my *back*.' That's how I got my check, $640 a month, plus my settlement, though my shyster's the one really made out."

"But we got our *home* out of it, Ernie," Sherry reminded him.

"Seeing you with that football," Dennis ventured, "I'd never have guessed—"

"I'm in agony every moment of every day," Ernie averred with a grimace. "My pain on the scale of 1 to 10? As I sit here, a good stout 9."

It developed that Sherry, too, received a monthly SSI check, on account of her fibromyalgia, not to mention asthma, that Bobby was hers and not theirs, and also that she and Ernie weren't married but engaged, and had chosen RV life for the unpaid volunteer jobs it offered because they couldn't show income without losing their checks.

Maureen didn't know what to think, and perhaps as a consequence hit the Chablis harder than usual.

When Bobby demanded he set up the satellite dish, Ernie, belching, demurred.

The boy screamed so loud in response that Ernie grudgingly set himself to the task, bringing out a contraption like a David Smith sculpture and fine-tuning its aim at outer space—where red Mars was pursuing thin white Diana, the moon—in response to shouts from indoors. Success achieved, bursts of light and the basso rumble of explosions made clear that war was being waged inside the Beanblossom rig.

Percy happened to drive out. Pausing at the booth to sneer at Jack, he caught sight of the Beanblossoms and turned his square face to look over their encampment. Giving Jack a satirical two-fingered salute, he set his roof lights to flashing and pulled up behind the land yacht with a single dying whine of the siren. Getting out, groaning, he moved to Dennis's picnic table, holding his arms out as though to facilitate a quick draw.

The motorhome erupted with Diego barking and Bobby shouting, "SHUT UP! SHUT UP!"

"Hey, Percy," slurred Dennis, "like a beer?"

Percy didn't accept. Beer was in ample evidence on Dennis's picnic table, but Percy did as the rangers did if they happened to like someone, keeping his eyes at face level so as to see nothing he had to correct or report.

"Want to welcome you folks to Fort Horace State Park," he said after Dennis introduced him. The Beanblossoms sat still and quiet, faces flashing yellow from his lights. "We're easy-going here. Very few rules. But infractions will not be tolerated. Hear a dog barking inside that rig. Barking will not be tolerated. And a kid: Don't tell me that kid's on summer vacation already?"

"My son is home-schooled by myself," Sherry announced. "If he gets a summer vacation, it will be a short one in August. Bobby has ADHD, if you must know."

"Home-schooled, eh?" Percy had a record of success in siccing truant officers on park residents' children; home-schooling was the one sure way to balk him. "Well, just so it's on the up and up. Dennis, any trouble, let me know, 24/7."

"Sure thing, Percy."

And Percy turned around and made his way to his truck with the gait that allowed his legs to clear his balls, *just*. Killing his roof lights, he backed up and drove out.

Ernie snarled, "Fuck he think he is? Lucky I didn't get in his face."

Traffic had ceased. From the booth Jack could hear the hum of the Interstate a few miles to the north, sounding purposeful but lonely.

Dennis strolled over to suggest he knock off early, so Jack posted Percy's signs, switched off the lights and exchanged his meager receipts for a beer. Finally Ernie and Sherry, belching, smacking their lips contentedly, linked arms and made unsteady progress across the grass to their rig, and Dennis got his keys to run Maureen and Maggie home. First he had to wake up Maureen, snoring over her spilled glass of Chablis.

Jack rode along.

## 12.

ERNIE BEANBLOSSOM classed himself for all time, so far as Maureen was concerned, the day she watched from the booth as a possum or raccoon came up from the gully at the curve and crossed the road. She worried about it until it reached the pavement's edge. Then she relaxed.

At that instant the Beanblossom van appeared, yanked onto the shoulder and flattened the creature. Ernie got out and swung it by its tail into the back. Wiping his hands on his shirt, he came on again, cheerily giving extra toots to his horn as he turned into his site.

What he barbecued that night she didn't want to know. After eating whatever it was, he sat in high contentment at Dennis's fire, shirtless, beer in hand, eyes a little watery.

The Beanblossoms rapidly established themselves as a source of delightful outrage to everybody in the park.

No one embraced disorder so instinctively, as their very element, as did the Beanblossoms. To see their site's transformation over a short course of days was to witness order descend into chaos—entropy in fast-forward. The queenly old motorhome—which by daylight had her issues: paint faded, peeling and scratched, her voluptuous curves outlined in rust, a distinct list—presided over an array of junk that spread out from day to day: broken tricycles, broken lawnmowers, broken wheelbarrows, broken chainsaws, broken and outmoded computers, TVs, cassette players, VCRs, radios, broken tables, broken beds, broken toasters, broken dolls.

Soon junk carpeted an acre as though a tornado had hit. But Ernie and Sherry continued to develop their enterprise on a colossal scale.

For enterprise it was. Sherry liberally handed out business cards that read (anticipating slightly, of course) "Ernie and Sherry Beanblossom, *Joyous RV Christians.*" Then got to the point: "FREE HAULING."

They were entrepreneurs: They would take away, forever, anything anyone wanted to be rid of, and do it without charge. They provided this service not only because it was the Christian thing to do, but because it allowed them to get something for nothing, something they could then sell for whatever the market would bear.

Something? *Everything!*

Every morning they set out in the Astro, flatbed in tow, in response to FREE HAULING requests received via cellphone, text and email, and to make the rounds of every garage sale, yard sale, rummage sale, estate sale, swap meet, auction and sheriff's execution within 20 miles, not to buy—never to *buy*—but to carry off—for FREE—the unsold and unsalable, the damaged and junked, the unneeded, the abandoned, the unloved, the detritus. Bring it home to turn into gold. Their eyes flashed at every thought of FREE.

On Fort Horace's bulk pick-up days they began early and finished late, triumphantly making multiple trips to bring back what no one else wanted. Some of it, after consideration, ended up at its original destination—the dump—but they never wasted even a trip *there*, for invariably they discovered treasures amidst the trash and returned to the park going slow, the springs of the van bottomed out with its load and the flatbed overflowing.

After Dennis relayed complaints about their field of possessions—the mowers were particularly aggrieved—the Beanblossoms rented a storage unit in town. Soon they added a second and a third. From her throne there—a braced folding chair, sinking into the ground—Sherry directed Ernie and Bobby in apportioning their acquisitions. Thereafter they brought home to store outdoors temporarily only those items in need of what Ernie called "minor repair" or "refinishing," tasks so trivial he never found time for them. Their plain of treasures spread out instead of shrinking, grass soon waving tall over everything.

The Beanblossoms knew that achieving wealth and status—life's whole point, after all—is merely a matter of reveling in enough *stuff*. They could not be deterred.

Maureen thought they had a point. In fact, the Beanblossoms operated as the most acute critics of American life she knew, collecting their disability checks while working incessantly on their social advancement. But it broke her heart to see the real sweat they worked up in amassing junk.

The flaw in their scheme was that it proved easier to amass than to sell. A tale of intolerance emerged: Through misunderstandings purely due to the inherent itinerancy of RV life, eBay banned Sherry's auctions. Other attempts at monetizing their possessions, whether through Craigslist or selling directly from the storage units, seldom netted a dime. That didn't daunt their sturdy hearts, however, which clearly lay in the collecting and not the selling.

Chaos accompanied the Beanblossoms into the booth, too. At first Sherry treated visitors to the warm and inviting, if lofty, presence of Eleanor Roosevelt. From that height she soon descended to become a tad more familiar, until Dennis had to ask her to stop calling everyone "dear" or "honey."

He also worked at improving her understanding of the different permits. Early on, when handed $50 for an Annual Permit, Sherry accidentally handed back a $25 *Second* Annual instead (purchasers of an Annual being entitled to buy another for a second vehicle at half price), and the extra $25 sank without trace into the maw of Dennis's bookkeeping forms. She was perplexed.

But she entered the booth early and stayed late, and that was what Dennis chiefly required. She used her shift to plumb the

## THE WEDDING ON BIG BONE HILL

wonders of the Internet. Wiring cellphone to laptop with what she proudly described as an illegal cable, she all day pushed at the keyboard, often not noticing visitors until they honked or rapped on the glass.

When the line grew long, she bawled for her better half and Ernie would shamble over to help out with a fistful of pre-marked daily passes and pockets stuffed with change.

But his twice-weekly source of cash—donating blood plasma, at $25 a session—tended to interfere with his performance. Having his blood ratcheted through tubes and filters left him with a disassembled, distracted air, not to mention gaudy bruises on his arms. Lurching up to a car like Frankenstein's monster, blinking and out of it, he would rest tattooed and bandaged forearms on the driver's sill and thrust his face inside, flashing his intensely white and even teeth, unless he forgot to put them in, in which case visitors saw more of his gums than they necessarily wished to.

They recoiled. More than one wittily remarked to Percy that, seeing Ernie approach, they expected him to extort a tip by washing the windshield.

Complaints rolled in one Saturday when he was especially woozy.

Percy radioed the booth. "Twenty-five to 54, everything OK out there? Ten-four."

"Everything's *swell*, Percy," Sherry answered. "How're things with *you*?" She let him hear her counting out change to a customer.

"S'Ernie doing OK? Ten-four."

"Ernie's *great!* Want to say hello?"

"Someone said he was drunk. Ten-four."

"That's from the blood loss, Percy. Hasn't touched a drop. Wish he would, they recommend it for donors."

"Twenty-five to 33," said Percy.

"Yo, Percy!" Dennis responded promptly. "This is 33."

"Dennis, suggest you check out your booth."

"That's a ten-four, Percy! Over and out!"

Dennis took over while Ernie went indoors to lie down.

Sherry suggested that Jack, too, earn extra cash by donating plasma. "Just lie there a couple hours watching TV," she told him, "and they hand you a five and a twenty."

"But is it the healthiest thing?" he asked.

"Absolutely no risk," Sherry assured him, scandalized at the notion. *"None.* Everything's sterile. Go with Ernie next time, just bring I.D. and answer 'No' to all their questions."

Sherry wished to donate, too, but the clinic wouldn't let her after she broke its big scale on her first visit, making it impossible to record her weight. She pointed out that they could easily use two ordinary bathroom scales to weigh her by adding the results. When they declined, she ridiculed the idiocy of the bureaucratic mind thus revealed, and they barred her from the premises altogether.

All in all, the Beanblossoms were in trouble from the day they arrived. As Maureen explained to Jack, "Park people hate the mess, hate the kid, hate how they treat the kid, hate the dog, hate how they treat the dog, and did I mention the mess?"

"But underneath everything," Jack offered, "don't you think they're doing the best they can?"

"Kansas can't take people like that," Maureen said tartly. "Kansas wants them *gone.*"

Her tone might have been due to a confidential chat Sherry took her aside for one day. Maureen thought herself too proud to care about Rumor until Sherry confided, "Heard about Percy dumping you, Maureen. Might not believe it *now,* but you'll get over it. But frankly, he's so mean when he's not getting any, be doing everybody a favor if you made up.

"So horny, he'll go for it, I'm sure."

## 13.

BIG BONE HILL'S burnt prairie grasses resurrected themselves as April wore on and gave way to May. First they tinted the scorched earth with a tender algae green and sent tentative shoots upwards. Then they exploded into jungle growth.

The rest of the park also blossomed. And visitors began to overrun it, especially on weekends making it resound with the glad sounds of America at play, notably with a nonstop *thump-thump-thump* from speedboats slapping the lake that kept dogs, particularly, on edge.

Maureen was working booth, and Dennis and Jack drinking at the fire ring—or Dennis drinking and Jack, who seldom had more than a couple of beers, nursing his first—when the Beanblossoms returned with their day's haul, coming up the lane with silver trumpets blaring a triumphant charge.

Broken floor lamps poked out of the van's windows, and the flatbed overflowed with flotsam and jetsam: broken file cabinets, broken fans, a torn movie screen, half a croquet set, a cash register *sans* drawer and, like a skinny ancient river god riding a life raft, clinging to the neck of a guitar as though it were a life preserver, a bare-chested young man in shorts and sneakers. The muscles of his torso and long hairy legs plated and pulled as, looking out alertly from beneath a mop of dark hair, he fought to stay afloat.

When Ernie parked, the newcomer jumped off and helped unload. No introductions were offered; after everything was dispersed in the tall grass Ernie and Sherry and Bobby herded the castaway into the land yacht.

Jack and Dennis looked at each other with surmise.

Soon a face darkened the porthole in the motorhome's door,

and the young man emerged, guitar strapped to his shoulder. Still shirtless, he paused at the bottom of the chrome steps to shove his cut-offs lower on his slender hips so that—as he swam over smiling, putting out his hand and saying, "Hey, how's it goin'? I'm *Rick*"—there showed above them a horizon of pubic hair.

They were charmed. Jack shook his limp hand, Dennis placed a beer in it. When Rick threw back his head and drank, his nipple ring bounced over a tattoo of the crazed jalopy driver whose steering wheel it represented. Sitting down cocked towards Jack, he assumed a succession of dynamic poses. Bowing forward made his vertebrae so press against his skin as almost to pop out, but lifting his beer and throwing his head back compressed them the other way. Whenever a car went past he gave a long roadward glance, shoulders heroically torqued.

Jack and Dennis drank in every variation of his posture, as did Ernie and Bobby when they joined them.

Shortly after Maureen closed the booth and crossed to the campfire, Percy veered into Dennis's site. He sat staring for a minute as Rick played chords before he climbed down, groaning, and shocked Dennis by saying, "Hey, Denny, got a cold one for me?"

Percy accepted the beer, but stood off from the table, watching Rick—watched him straight out and steady, not pretending to do anything else, except curl his lip. Rick gazed innocently back through his fringe. His strumming underscored the distant highway whine.

"Going to put on a shirt?" Percy finally asked.

"I'm too hot," Rick said.

"Say that again," Dennis mumbled.

"Guess we're wondering where you washed up from?"

"California," Rick returned promptly.

"What brings you here, driftin'?"

"Travelin', yeah. See the USA."

"How'd you meet the Beanblossoms?"

"BOBBY!" Sherry bawled from the motorhome. "IT'S SPONGEBOB!"

That question about how they met never got an answer all summer. The presumption was that someone wanted Rick no longer, put him out on the curb with the broken vacuum cleaner.

"Old are you?"

"Twenty-two."

"Graduate high school?"

"No."

"I.D.?"

It was produced and studied.

Percy was working up to something. He handed back the driver's license and set a foot on the bench. His face slackening, he bent forward and slipped an edge of warmth into his voice like a shiv: "Got a record, don't you, boy?" He leaned back generously. "Hey, s'OK, everyone knows I got one myself. Long as you're not wanted?"

"No, sir."

"What is it?"

"California second-class felony. Expunged after seven years. Four to go."

"Can't be that bad, then. What you do?"

Bending his head back in a way that reminded Maureen of a fledgling swallowing a worm, Rick finished his beer and sat up straight.

"Cops stopped me for a burned-out license-plate light, busted me for my homemade renewal tag."

"My land!" she said, not meaning to. "Seven years' banishment for *that*?"

"Yes, ma'am."

In that huge night landscape Percy made a funny sound, pitched high: He was laughing. Had himself a good one. So did the others, of course. No one wanted to be left out. Rick looked gloomy.

"Well, well, dangerous character," Percy said. "Have to watch out for *you*. Know what *I* did?"

"Heard about it."

"So we don't want no shit going down, right?"

"No, sir."

"One of those things, pay a fine, get out from under?"

"Where am I going to get 3,000 bucks?"

"Job, maybe?" Percy said with a sneer. "Crap job like felons get, only *your* first $3,000 clears your record?"

"Go to college, have any kind of life you want," Jack put in eagerly.

Rick reached for a beer.

"You like girls?"

"Yes, sir!"

"'*Yes, sir!*'" Percy mocked. "'Sure, you *betcha!*' Well, *that's* a novelty, around *here*. Just keep your ass wiped and your nose clean."

Setting down his untouched can with the report of a judge's gavel, Percy left, climbing into his truck with a groan, raking them with the headlights and driving away.

Rick sat collapsed, his shoulder blades reproachful, like broken wings. From behind, Ernie tousled his hair and gave him a hug.

"Hey, pardner, don't let that asshole get to you. *Asshole*. Lucky I didn't get in his face!"

## 14.

MAY PASSED, and they were in June.

As springtime progressed, the evening skies began to mix explosive ingredients, and severe-weather alerts came almost daily. Storms shedding lightning bolts moved in with a rumble as of pillars being pulled down, and many an evil-looking cloud dragged black teats overhead. Half a dozen times Maureen had the cats crated and ready to go. Even as tornadoes swept past—one demolished a two-story apartment house on the near side of town—they shunned the park itself, though whenever the megaphone-shaped speaker in the middle of the campground revolved shrieking atop its pole, Jack, to his own eyes pathetic, donned his bicycle helmet and watched outdoors apprehensively.

Jack proved popular in the booth. Visitors liked the way he dealt with them. He was the warm if slightly dizzy provider of too much information; even his innovative, somewhat un-Kansan *"Welcome"* went over. He pressed brochures and maps on visitors with abandon, greeted their kids, welcomed their dogs, even lent free passes to first-time visitors wishing to take a look around.

He was attentive, accurate, fecund of suggestion—where to find shade, where to find quiet, where to find groupers or perch—and behind it all, standing there in the little room, windows open, classical or country music playing, a book open before him, keeping up with the continental panorama and infused with joy.

But sometimes, especially when he was trying to cope with the Friday afternoon rush—vehicles arriving in clumps governed by the stoplights in town—the radio would crackle, "Twenty-five to 54," and Percy would order him to close the booth and come to the ranger station for a minute.

"Jack, guy came in with another complaint about you," Percy told him on one such occasion. "Says he flipped his badge, but you made him buy a daily. I had to buy it back."

"I know who you mean: Investigator with the Emporia prosecutor's office? Asked if he was here on official business, and he said no."

"Jack, anyone connected to law enforcement—and I mean *anyone*—gets in free. They show you a badge or a card, or tell you their cousin's wife's neighbors' boss's son used to be a cop in *Podunk*, they get in free. That simple."

"Money out of the State's pocket, and Dennis's."

"You just won't understand the way we do business here, will you?"

And in the campground, several times a week Jack could count on seeing the squared-off old truck sweep through the loops the wrong way, Percy's wide sneer aimed at him. The loops were one-way, but Percy drove them in the wrong direction, the better to come upon infractions. He would pull up near Jack's site, sometimes turning off his engine and watching until at some unseen cue he moved off again.

Also there came what felt like surveillance from the rangers as Jack encountered them at odd times and places. Two evenings running, Ranger Ray parked near the boat ramps while Jack and Lady watched the sun fall into the lake, and sat watching *them*. Jack noticed a certain knowing lift of Ranger Ray's lip, a wrinkle of Ranger Randy's nose whenever, on bicycle or on foot, he met their trucks or ATVs.

Well, the whole country was under surveillance. One could no longer even board an airplane without first gesturing *I surrender*. It made Jack feel especially self-conscious whenever he happened to ride through the Picnic Park, for with his first swing through he recognized it as a lover's lane, and soon realized that the gazebo was tacitly set aside for cruising. But he merely pedaled onward.

Meanwhile he established what felt like an indefinitely sustainable routine. Daylight hours he spent outdoors reading—issued a Fort Horace library card, he borrowed books by the packful—and giving Lady long walks. They were covering ten miles a day and more, and thriving on it, though the plenitude of deer ticks required that Jack, returning indoors, strap his ankles with duct tape to lift off the tiny smudges, and keep close watch on Lady's coat, too.

## 15.

RICK JOINED with a will in the Beanblossom enterprise. Alongside Ernie he sweated wrestling broken freezers out of people's garages and hauling cartons of moldy magazines up cellar steps. Under Sherry's discriminating eye he helped pack everything into the storage units or strew it over the grass.

Then he, too, pressed a cold can of Dennis's Old Milwaukee to his forehead while looking over the field of junk with Ernie's own pride, farmers sowing what promised to be a rich harvest.

He also joined in donating plasma. Ernie loved having Rick in the next chaise lounge while watching *Oprah*, "like we're on a fucking cruise." And he cherished their leaving woozily together: "Like tying it on with your best friend." Coming home one day, arms bruised and bandaged, sharing a mental vagueness, each the richer by $25, on impulse Ernie darted into a salon and blew their earnings on a dye job. Emerging with his locks dyed gold, he thereafter moved with a consciousness of youth and beauty regained.

One evening Rick, eyes burning a little deeper than usual, strummed his guitar beneath Mars's pursuit of Diana, until—urged on by Ernie—he began to sing. He rendered an achingly sincere

*Home on the Range* in a richly shaded baritone, following it with *I'm So Lonesome I Could Cry*. Everyone applauded.

"Rick, that's a gift!" said Maureen.

"I'm the next George Strait!" he answered.

"No, really, you're good," said Dennis.

"The new Garth Brooks!"

"Don't put yourself down, Rick," Ernie commanded. "You're *good*."

"Really," said Jack.

Every campfire thereafter burned to underlying chords and a song or two.

And every evening after Rick stepped out of the land yacht in his skinny near-nudity and paused to shove his shorts down his hips—clearly only the bulge at the front held them up—Jack watched the different plays for his favor.

Ernie paid dogged court, fetching repellant as needed and, when he barbecued—expertly—pressing the choicest morsels on Rick, at the same time claiming him with a hand on his shoulder.

Dennis he inspired to a running joke about needing a houseboy and being willing to audition him for the job. Often while Rick strummed, Dennis would be working the kinks out of his smooth back, kneading his way down to the tufted small of it and up again, making him groan contentedly (and in key), until Ernie whined, "Don't *I* get any?"

In Sherry he induced girlish yipping laughter that made flesh jiggle all over.

Diego *adored* Rick. Morning and evening, Rick took him out of his portable kennel and let the dog whipsaw him like a stick figure down the road and back (Bobby followed, pedaling a bike with monkey bars and banana seat, frolicking and caracoling—anything to get Rick's attention). When Rick relaxed at Dennis's picnic table, the dog would set to pushing his chain-link enclosure across the grass (making Maggie and Lady nervous), until it was proverbial that, "When you see the fire in Diego's eyes, time to pack it in."

Jack meanwhile also entered the race for Rick's affections. He kept it low key, even ironic, trying to be pleasant and supportive, but in fact he was more ambitious than anyone else, even though he *never* chased straight men: He doubted that Rick was really *straight*.

Maureen alone was unaffected by Rick, except with the dismay a young person adrift can inspire in his elders.

Each who paid Rick homage received recognition freely bestowed. Bobby got his roughhousing, held upside down or arms pinioned behind his back. At the close of an evening Ernie had a store of unblinking looks to savor; Dennis retained the springy feel of his flesh; Sherry could review his shy answering laughs, and Jack the whole spectacle.

One evening, looking as though it pained him, Rick sang a lyric of his own:

> *When the stars go swimmin' in slo-mo*
> *Through the oceans overhead,*
>
> *Are we driftin', driftin', driftin',*
> *Or pulled to destiny?*

Nothing additional floating into his ken, he repeated:

> *Are we driftin', driftin', driftin',*
> *Or pulled to destiny?*

## 16.

EARLY ON one of her shifts, the towering silver clouds scudding in like pirate ships made Maureen nervous. To try to take her mind off the sky, she cleaned up the booth as if it was her own house, fancying as she sprayed glass and wiped counters that the clouds scraping overhead emitted a rumble too deep to hear.

In the course of her marriage she'd presided over two houses.

The first one she and her husband moved into after their honeymoon, a pavilion of concrete block and glass designed by an architect who apprenticed with Frank Lloyd Wright and built many such homes in the region, especially in the declivities that mark the Fort Horace River's search for the Missouri.

Maureen found it a deeply satisfying place to live. It was made up of a series of lofty spaces open to the seasons off a low entry hall. She became accustomed to effects of light arresting her until the sun made some distinct alteration in its position and the effect dissolved.

They sold that house and moved into town after her husband inherited his mother's mansion, a three-story mountain of stone built in the 1890s. The roiling, energetic Romanesque mass was replete with arches and pilasters and a tower crowned by a slate cone topped with a rock ball. Twenty-four dark rooms swallowed up Mother's *objets d'art* and suites of furniture, some given her at her marriage by her wheat-king father, and gaped for more.

It was such a jumble of ugly stuff—graceless proportions, chunky machine carving, peeling veneers—Maureen could hardly stand it. But she had to. Every piece, every stick spoke to her husband from his childhood and thus was sacred.

Her life thereafter was a long arc of service to the care of house and contents: scraping, painting, varnishing, waxing, polishing. Never done. Whereas the modern house had been a weightless container for light and shade, mood and emotion, the old house's monumentality weighed on her. The only thing that could arrest her in *it* was the conviction, ultimately inescapable, that she'd married the wrong man.

When he suddenly died—"his heart throbbed one morning," she once heard herself explain—she sold the drafty edifice and its contents with a haste that scandalized her friends, moved into the trailer and pulled it to the park. The buyers were a young couple who frowned at her inauthentic treatments.

Maybe too long a time living in a house that represented aspiration—but not hers—was what made Maureen content to live in a box on wheels. Or maybe it was finding her head suddenly gray, extruding filament spun from bone, skeleton made visible, that had her mad to try a new life; as women do, she blamed aging on her own negligence. In any case, after moving into the park she made a happy investigation of red rinses, finding they went with her high Irish cheekbones.

Polishing the booth's windows, she was shaken out of her reverie when the weather radio came alive with emergency tones, followed by a voice speaking from the bottom of a well: "The National Weather Service in Kansas City has issued a tornado alert for Barber County."

She flipped on the booth's tiny RV TV to find the screen mapping panicky green over the countryside while type too small to read rushed along the bottom. A cheerful young weatherman bobbed in front of the radar image, saying with the warmth of a car salesman, "Touchdowns reported near the state park west of Fort Horace, no confirmation yet, but radar shows the front spawning numerous areas of rotation."

He induced in Maureen, exposed in the glass-walled shack, a first stirring of panic, but she knew what to do: change channels and find her favorite weatherman, warm, imperturbable and black. By contrast with the other, he conveyed acceptance that no one knew what might happen in the next hour, or could avert it, but also faith that together they would endure it.

She calmed down, and soon so did the sky.

And in that calm, she found herself thinking about Percy, the man of her trailer house.

For the first time, their affair struck her as a diminishment of herself—less than what self-respect demanded. Though on the one hand she missed him—and could locate on her body just where—on the other, a veil, not of shame, exactly, but *regret* was descending that she'd accepted a man so not warm, so impenetrable, for any sort of exchange, much less for the personal, intimate kind—*supposedly* intimate kind—they'd performed.

In retrospect, it was less a workable, grown-up arrangement than a betrayal of herself.

When traffic died she took her receipts over to Dennis, but for once declined his offer of wine and went home. There was Chablis in her fridge.

A tornado indeed descended that evening, smashing to matchsticks the Picnic Park pavilion next up from the gazebo.

## 17.

THAT NIGHT PERCY made another flashlight patrol of the campground. Squatting beside Jack's rig, he flicked his beam over its chassis. To his disappointment everything still seemed in order.

But as he was rising, effortfully squelching his groan, his flashlight hit pay dirt at last. Darting it around, he came up with the heady grand total of six infractions: Count 'em, *six!* Smacking his lips, he got to his feet with a pull on the rig that set it to rocking and the dog to barking furiously. From pure joy he gave it a thump for good measure. *Had him now.*

The next day, Mark putting in a rare morning at the ranger station, Percy waylaid him at his desk, looming in the doorway, barring egress, waiting for him to hang up the phone. His propensity for doing so might have been one reason for the rarity of Mark's office visits.

When at length Mark finished arranging his vacation schedule with Pratt, home of the Kansas parks agency, Percy started in. First he pointed out how the new Vendor system meant Dennis was raking in the big bucks. A high-season Saturday might see 1,500 or 2,000 vehicles coming in, and perhaps half would buy a daily pass: From each, a buck for the Vendor. $1,000 for *Dennis?*

"Tell me about it," said Mark, not looking up.

"I could do the job, all I'm saying."

"Law says no felons."

"You testified in Topeka, you could get it changed."

"And cook my goose? My job's all politics, Percy. I know you *know* that, but sometimes I think you don't appreciate how that ties my hands."

Percy guessed he at least had Mark in a more conducive frame of mind for his other concern.

"Listen, took a look at that faggot's motorhome. We got a problem."

"We do if you keep calling him that, Percy."

"What?" Percy was bewildered.

"He has a name. *Not* the one you called him."

"He's also got six split rims on that old rig of his. Ever seen one blow? Take your head clean off!"

"Well, I doubt Jack's going to be fooling with his tires."

"Can't register a vehicle with split rims in Kansas, Mark."

"That may be, but he's registered in California. Look, Percy, if we went after every little thing, there'd be no end. Split rims are no big deal compared to the old propane tanks, but—"

"Grandfathered in," Percy pointed out. "And it's against the law to fill them."

"Sure, but people do it. QuikeeBuy does it if no one's around. One of these days some rusted-out old valve will blow us all to kingdom come. Personally, I don't care about the rims, but thanks for telling me."

He nodded crisply, but Percy didn't budge.

"*What?*"

"Just saying, want to get rid of this fa—*gay*—the rims'll do as well as anything else."

Mark's eyes flashed. "Like your job, Percy?"

Percy drew himself up, sneering.

"Regardless whether I like it or—"

"Because here on in, *I* don't pay your salary, *Dennis* does. You have to understand, this new law changes everything. Used to be *us* that pulled in the money and sent it off to Pratt? No more. The new law says the *Vendor* recruits, trains, staffs the booth, orders permits as needed, gets the receipts in, and for that he gets his slice. And Dennis is the Vendor.

"Oh, I know, it's only when the booth's open, April through September, we still get the self-pay and the ones who walk in here. But like it or not, on an annual basis it'll be 70, 75% Dennis. And Dennis hired Jack."

"But—"

"And there's this to put in the mix, too, Percy: I know Mrs. Godwin did the best she could when she ran the booth, bless her. And God knows I appreciate the time you spent with her, *trying* to make sense of her accounts."

For once, Mark was looking directly at Percy, who actually took a step back, until he caught himself and stepped forward again.

"Now all that's Dennis's problem. But for whatever reason, what Dennis sends Pratt month by month this summer will likely run— Oh, I don't know, what's *your* guess? Ten per cent more? Fifteen per cent more? Maybe a *quarter* more than last year?"

Mark waited until Percy's mouth opened before he resumed.

"*A quarter again as much,* Percy? It ain't hay. Might even say it makes you wonder. Might even make 'em wonder in *Pratt.* Let's hope all the parks send that much more in, don't want heat coming down on *us.*" Lowering his head and shuffling papers, he said more accommodatingly, "Look, if Jack raises your hackles like this, must be something about him."

"He's mouthy, thinks he's better than we are, and—"

"Happy to come down on him like a ton of bricks, but there has to be a *reason.* Catch him *in flagrante* or something."

Percy liked the sound of what Mark was saying, but had no actual idea of what he meant.

"In— In *what?*"

"Find him doing whatever—soliciting, beating off in the showers, anything like that, and he's *out* of here. See him take little boys into his motorhome, call the cops."

"You got it," said Percy, accepting the commission.

But the upshot was mixed. His crusade against Jack had suddenly taken on an anxious tinge of self-preservation.

## 18.

NEXT DAY Maureen was visiting at Charlene's, sitting in the shade at her picnic table. Charlene's grandson Brendan was inside the trailer, watching television, and Chuck was out on the lake.

Percy's truck crunched over the gravel. He stepped out holding a clipboard. Aviator sunglasses deepened the amber of his eyes.

"'Lo, ladies," he said.

"Percy," said Charlene with the caution he usually elicited.

"Who's manning the station?" Maureen asked.

"Mark thought he'd put in an honest hour's work for a change," Percy said, not looking at her.

"Will wonders never cease."

"Charlene, OK if I sit down?"

"Please."

"Won't take up much of your time. Just checking out a situation. Kind you want to nip in the bud if there's anything not on the up and up."

"What is it, Percy?"

"Like to talk to Brendan, you don't mind."

Maureen could see behind the screen door the silhouette of a young head turning.

"What's he done?"

"Hasn't done anything."

"It'll have to be in front of me."

"Fine. One question first."

"You don't need me," Maureen said.

"You stay right there, Maureen," Charlene told her.

"Just trying to make sure Brendan hasn't been led into an inappropriate—*ah*—friendship." Maureen saw panic in Charlene's eyes, and knew Percy saw it too. Sometimes Maureen hated that man. "There's a new volunteer this year, name of Jack. Know him? Works booth?"

"Sure, we know Jack," Charlene said. She silently sucked in a breath. "We like him."

"He take up with Brendan in any way?"

"No. They've met. Jack's been over for roast corn. And fish. But they're not especially—"

"Mind if we go in and see him?"

"Brendan!"

"Yes, Nana?"

"Come out a minute, please."

Brendan came out, blinking at the sun, and joined them at the picnic table.

Status was at work. Like Maureen, Chuck was a volunteer, but his job cleaning the boat-landing restrooms put him at the bottom of the heap. That he never asked Travis if he needed another mower, never looked into being a painter or working booth, perhaps indicated how easy it was to go down to the marina twice a week to wipe and mop and restock the men's and ladies', but those who mowed or painted or worked booth looked down on him.

Whether Chuck cared, no one knew, but Charlene certainly did. And this without any consideration that their daughter had borne a black child.

"*Hey*-ya, Brendan, how's it going?" Percy said through his teeth.

"Hi," Brendan replied.

"Now, you're not in any kind of trouble, none whatsoever. Telling your grandmother here, just looking out for her grandbaby, that's all. You're at that age where— How old are you?"

"Sixteen next month."

"That right? Got your growth, though. What time you get up in the morning?"

"Nana?" asked Brendan in bewilderment.

"Nine or 10:00," she said. "It's summer."

"And take a shower first thing? Go to the showerhouse?"

"Yes?"

"Anyone there the same time? Residents, you know, they have jobs to go to, and visitors want to get on the water, they'll be out of there by 7:30, 8:00 o'clock—*early*. Ten o'clock, who else you see in there?"

"You're kidding, right?"

"This guy Jack— You know Jack?
"Yes."
Now Percy had his pen walking across the clipboard.
"Gets up around the same time, don't he?"
"No idea."
"No, Brendan? You don't know what time Jack gets up?"
"Why should I?"
"Because we hear he's in the showerhouse when you are, mornings. That's the report *we* get."
"Who tells you that?" asked Charlene.

Percy just grinned.

"Percy, what are you insinuating?" Charlene pressed with the asperity any grandmother should have at her command.

"Nothing, Charlene. Give us a minute here." Percy turned a page. "Brendan: Jack ever walk in on you in the showers?"

"No, sir."

"Ever make *suggestions* to you—?"

"No, sir."

"—or walk around stark naked in front of you—?"

"No, sir!"

"—holding his business?"

"*Never.*"

"Shown himself off to you naked, though, hasn't he? Maybe said why don't you get together, you and him? Come over, show you his motorhome?"

"Never seen him naked."

"Percy, this has gone—"

Percy tapped his clipboard. "Never *saw*, or never *looked*—?"

Brendan stood up, and so did Charlene.

"*Never!*"

"Percy!"

"Hey, got a report," said Percy, snapping his pen and working to his feet. "Mark said check it out, that's all. Nothing to do with your young man, Charlene. But you don't want this Jack character abusing anyone, do you?"

"No."

"Well, he's new here, we don't know him, he may be all right — but frankly, we just have a feeling." Percy turned to Brendan. "So listen, son, this guy get friendly, let us know, OK? *Me*, personally, right away."

Brendan spat, "Nana, I'm going inside." And did so.

"Percy Bratcher, you ought to be ashamed of yourself," Maureen said, "coming down here and saying such—"

"Has to be done, Maureen, 'less you want the worst to happen. Charlene, just let me know if Jack does anything... *queer*." His lips enjoyed how the word pulled his mouth into a rictus. "Don't want a situation we could have caught in time. I thank you both for your time. Ladies."

"Hold on," Charlene said tersely, and went indoors. A minute later she came out with a paper sack filled with butternut squash and early tomatoes.

When fruits and vegetables begin to pile up people will overlook what they can. It was the time of year when everyone who knew anyone with a farm or garden labors under gifts of produce; the time of plenty everyone looks forward to the rest of the year, never remembering that when it comes it's a bit of a trial.

"From my sister's."

"Why, thank you kindly."

Looking pleased with himself, Percy swaggered with the sack to his truck, groaned his way up into it, backed out and drove off.

Charlene sat simmering. "There goes the creepiest man in Fort Horace," she said.

Then they looked over at Jack's motorhome, jammed beneath a maple whose new draperies the slow breeze sighed to silver.

That evening Chuck dropped Brendan off at his mother's in Kansas City.

## 19.

JACK OBSERVED THAT, as weather alerts were the soundtrack to April and May, so were the melodies of the mowers to June. They accompanied the growth that erupted as the sun lingered longer every day. Big Bone Hill went from growth ankle high to riotous skyward vegetation. In walking Lady up the zigzag path that Travis personally mowed every week, he could hardly see over the greenery to either side, it was so like a tunnel.

This was Travis's high season, when, somnolent as a reptile the rest of the year, seldom seen but sitting—as with many American men of 65 or 70, it pained him to stand or walk for any ordinary chore—he every day hoisted himself onto his charger's soft-sprung seat and commenced single combat with the grass.

His crew of eight won their positions by first putting years in at other volunteer jobs. Mowing was considered the most desirable of them all. They rated machines according to seniority, from Travis's full-size John Deere tractor, to the sit-down mowers, the self-powered standing mowers, the push mowers and the newest guy's weed-whacker.

Each was required to work only two days a week, but such is the siren call and deep satisfaction of mowing that every machine was in use every available hour. Bent beneath wide-brimmed hats, they swept in loose tag-team fashion on what seemed to Jack a Tolstoyan scale across meadows and campground and the verges of the road, drawing together only to consult or refuel. Their whirr and grind was constant, dawn to dusk, even as they began to lose the war they fought so heroically.

At the end of May the park was green and trim, grateful to the eye and gently accommodating to the feet. But then loveliness went awry. After rising reluctantly through mist, the sun burned all day and into the evening, hanging at its zenith for hours and hours, until finally the horizon caught it with nets of magenta and crimson.

In response the grass surged upwards. The grass grew too fast for Travis and his crew to keep up with. Even as the days went out of shape, so did the meadows.

Travis did his best. Still vibrating from the day before, at sunrise he mounted his mighty John Deere's saddle, swigged water, pulled his hat low and got going on those slopes and banks where the dew dried first. The sun would be only a hair's breadth above the horizon before he was yanking his blades over the ground.

He mowed—grim, determined, withal joyous—through the morning and long afternoon, at noon merely throttling back to eat the sandwich his wife packed for him. As the sun slowly lost heat and he worked through the long suspense of the end of the day, he felt he was waking up, coming alive. Turning on the Deere's bug-eyed headlights, he stole a march on the sun in his iconic, futile fight beneath the mighty sky, pioneering through tall grass, leaving it short, uniform, releasing fragrance that trailed him as sweetly as the susurration of his rolling blades.

Once on his tractor, Travis didn't get off; not unless to pee or refuel or unfoul his blades, or to kill a rattlesnake.

The sight of a rattler made him quiver as if shocked. He would steer for it in a quicksilver maneuver and grease his blades with its blood, leave strips of snakeskin wriggling on the ground. But in case the blades failed, he carried a machete on clips beside his engine. Machete in hand, he would scramble off his seat, lent agility by his purpose, and give chase.

When his prey coiled and shook its rattles—inaudibly because of the chugging tractor—he would swipe at it, send its head flying, flay its flesh across the grass. He had triumphs even greater, when he chased a rattler to find it gone to ground with its fellows; massacre would ensue. Officially, like all park wildlife, rattlesnakes were protected, but tacitly Travis had the go-ahead to kill on sight.

Ecstasy past, he would climb painfully back into his seat, having enacted the deepest meaning in life he knew. His obsession came not from the biblical injunction against the serpent—indeed, one day he spent a perilous half hour untangling a copperhead from a plastic six-pack carrier; he had nothing against copperheads—but from the vow he made when his son at the age of six was bitten by a rattlesnake on his ranch across the Oklahoma border from Caney, Kansas, and died convulsing in his arms.

He and his wife had long ago sold that sad ranch. But he carried on with his mission, keeping no count of his kills, collecting no rattles, but satisfied that he'd freed Earth of generations of rattlers that would otherwise infest it.

Only when the sun's afterglow faded did Travis finally go home, quench his tractor's yellow eyes and switch off the engine. After some shuffling protests, some stray firings, it stopped and he stiffly levered himself off and into his camper, and peace at last descended on the park.

But many—Jack among them—felt it was the *noise* of mowing that brought peace, was redolent of long summer days, and that it was when Travis shut his tractor *off* that peace was lost to the uneasy cries of coyotes and TVs and the sounds like caged lions that came from I-70.

## 20.

SOON AFTER the Fourth of July, Dennis stumbled outdoors one morning pasty-faced and hollow-eyed, and instead of going to work, hitched his truck to his trailer, jerked it out of its spot and left it at the side of the road.

With help from Rick and Bobby—Ernie postponed the day's hauling—he began emptying it. As they finished, a big rig came up the road caught in the jaws of an enormous white whale—on closer view, a gleaming new fiberglass fifth-wheel trailer 40 feet long. Aiming its bite away from the road, the crew positioned it where the trailer had been, smoothed the gravel, leveled the jacks, attached the umbilicals, opened the slide-outs and hauled the old rig away, while Dennis oversaw the transfer of his possessions into the new one.

That evening everybody got the grand tour.

"It's a McMansion!" Maureen exclaimed. The slide-outs made the rooms as large as a house's. It had oak floors, walnut bookshelves, granite counters, a fireplace, washer/dryer, garden tub, king-size bed, flat-screen TVs and built-in satellite dish.

"This is *amazing*," said Sherry. "But we would have taken your old one, you know."

"Trade-in," Dennis said.

"That booth must be a gold mine!" said Maureen.

"Nothing comes in November through March, remember, but trailer payments come due every month."

"Can your truck even pull this thing?" asked Jack.

"Getting a bigger one next month," Dennis snapped. "Believe me, guys, I deserve my success."

The Beanblossoms might have felt put out, except that fate—or the U.S. Government—smiled on them, too, that day: The mail brought an SSI check made out to Sherry for a cool $5,000.

By evening half was gone in a Walmart shopping spree, the

prize purchase being a plasma TV. They also brought home boxes of pizza from Chuck E. Cheese and pressed slices on everybody.

"*Five thousand dollars?*" Maureen asked. "Why ever *for?*"

Sherry's eyes went vague. "They've owed me a long time," she answered. "Took forever to start my check, so it's making up for that."

"Are you *sure?* No notation?"

"Just a rock-solid Government check, Maureen. Walmart cashed it without blinking an eye."

"Shouldn't you hang on to the money till you find out what it's *for?* Might be a mistake."

Sherry's brows made a jigsaw mismatch. The question did not compute.

Ernie reported that what was left of the windfall would buy the oldest American dream of all: Over the Internet he made a down payment on land in Texas, three acres near the Arkansas border. They would head there at season's end.

"Dream of my whole life and my daddy's before me," he said, staring into the fire and pushing out his dentures with satisfaction. "Own my own land."

"But sight unseen?" Jack asked.

"Plenty of pictures on the website," Ernie assured him, "plus testimonials."

"We Googled it," Sherry explained. "Came up clean. Only thing is the trees need clearing. That's why I'm glad I've got three strong men."

Rick didn't react to hearing himself enlisted to spend the winter felling trees on Ernie's new domain.

"See, clear it this winter," said Ernie. "Wire it, bring in water, next summer open Beanblossom's RV Park, cash in *bigtime*. So Jack, want a cheap place to stay, come on down, help out."

"Thanks," Jack said. "Maybe I will look in."

Sherry grabbed Ernie. "Honey, we can afford to get *married.*"

They kissed to cheers and clapping. Rolling her eyes, Maureen put down her wine to join in, while Jack queried Mars as to how *his* pursuit was getting on. He also noticed Rick's lashes winking closed like a happy cat's.

The Beanblossoms soon retired indoors to watch wide-screen HD satellite.

Later, as the campfire died and only Jack remained, Dennis bent back his head, taking in his enormous new rig, and slurred, "And t'think it all com'sh from shucking dick."

"Paris is worth a Mass," Jack answered, "but whose would that be?"

Dennis hesitated, then told him.

"Last fall, my trailer was over on your loop?" he began. "Started with my empties."

At 18 a day, he explained, they piled up fast, and it wasn't done to discard them inside the park; its community of drinkers was agreed on that. Dennis's solution was to let 'em accumulate for a week, conscientiously stamp 'em flat, bag 'em, drive over to the Picnic Park and throw 'em in a dumpster there.

Even that he accomplished discreetly. Of a Saturday he'd park at a pavilion, and only after making sure he was alone and unobserved would he jump out and swing the bag in with its unmistakable clangor.

One Saturday as Dennis drove into the Picnic Park on his mission, Percy's castoff truck was coming out. They exchanged bored waves; Dennis knew Percy then only as the man he paid his site rent to, but dreaded any encounter with him, he seemed so to move within his own sinister atmosphere. He parked at a pavilion—not the gazebo, he made Jack understand, but one farther along. Not a minute later, before he had a chance to scope things out, a car parked next to his. It was Ranger Randy in his personal Malibu.

"Know Ranger Randy?" Dennis asked. "Dishiest guy ever to

put on a uniform?"

"With the blond hair like his head's shoved in front of a spotlight?" Jack answered. It was his impression also that Ranger Randy wasn't averse to having tribute paid.

Dennis suspected why Ranger Randy might be hanging out in civvies on a Saturday in the Picnic Park: as vice sting bait. The rangers, with Percy's occasional help, moonlighted on the Fort Horace police force's anti-vice efforts, enticing men to make advances in public places and hauling away those who did to be stamped forevermore as sex offenders. Though they more often operated their stings near campus, the Picnic Park was also a regular venue, and Randy the vice squad's star attraction.

But Dennis felt immune to the particular legal process he imagined to be in operation, for he had no intention of picking up Ranger Randy *(as if)*. And Randy had to know what *his* errand was.

So he got out, threw his cans in the dumpster with a happy clangor, and willingly hung at Randy's window, smoking and shooting the breeze. Dennis joshed him about what he was up to on a Saturday, and where was his girlfriend, anyway? Everything was copacetic.

Finally he stepped on his butt, said, "*See*-ya, Randy," got in his truck and started the engine.

"OK, Dennis, hold on a sec?" Randy called over and, scrambling out, arrested him for driving under the influence.

A breathalyzer showed Dennis legally drunk, but he was bailed out not too many hours later. He knew the drill; it was his third DUI. But he was a wreck, because for a third DUI Kansas mandated a year in prison. And he hadn't driven an inch! All he did was turn the key!

The unfairness rankled, and his life seemed over—he'd lose his job (assistant manager at a dollar store) as well as his driver's license, once out of prison have to live in town. But when he got back to his trailer he found taped to the door a note from Percy inviting him down to the Airstream for a chat.

He went, not knowing what to expect. Percy sat him down opposite his armchair on a green plaid couch piled with gun magazines, and told him how upset Mark was about his arrest. Mark liked him and so did he, and personally he wouldn't wish prison on a dog.

But as it happened there might be a way out. Under a new law, the park needed a Vendor—a bondable person with office skills— to run the entrance booth. Would Dennis be interested?

"I go, 'Great, can I run it from a cell at Lansing?'" Dennis told Jack. "And Percy says Mark got the paperwork back from the cops, play ball, state'll never hear about my arrest. We all make mistakes, Percy tells me, he's the living proof.

"I go, 'What about *you* for Vendor?'"

"What did he say?" asked Jack.

"He's like, 'Topeka's way ahead of you, no felons need apply.' Goes, 'So are you interested?'

"'Yeah, I'm interested.'

"'Then maybe we're in business,' he says kind of thoughtfully. Spreads his legs, frowns, switches his cigarette to his left hand so his right can go to work."

"No!" said Jack.

"*Mais oui*. Rubs that itch, begins to breathe. Meanwhile I'm thinking of prison. But the extra money, too. What's the big deal? So I go, 'Can I help you out there, Percy?'" Dennis laughed ruefully, then, looking startled, said severely, "Just that one time, you understand."

"Guess he was thinking of prison, too," Jack said. "No wonder our friend has it in for me."

Dennis nodded crisply. *Naturally* Jack inflamed Percy: Jack was *out*, whereas Dennis hewed to the more classic posture whereby everybody *knew about* him, but he *didn't push it in anyone's face*. When asked why he wasn't married, instead of Jack's affirmation,

"Because I'm gay," Dennis explained that he "just never found the right girl, I guess," if necessary hinting at a hurt so deep he could never love again—that is, answered however the questioner wished. But to be *out* threatened the sexuality, the masculinity of every male around.

Jack indicated the McMansion. "Anyway, hope it's worth it to you."

Dennis's eyes widened.

"Oh, yes," he said.

## 21.

IT DIDN'T RAIN during the month of July. The grass stopped growing; once cut, it stayed cut, turning brown, stiff and crackly. That silenced the mowers; they were relegated to trimming trees, transplanting shrubs and killing poison ivy.

Meanwhile the sun hung at its apogee long into the night. The days never ended, and during the brief darkness Mars ceased to close the distance with Diana. The air stopped moving. Nothing made headway. Stasis embraced the park, and gradually so did an unwelcome smell.

At first it was a fugitive scent—an occasional *I hope I'm not smelling what I think I'm smelling.* Then it became an underlying presence. Finally the stench grew pervasive and nauseating.

The settlement ponds across a berm from the campground were more full of human waste than at any other time of the year. Every day fleets of RVs pulled off the Interstate to pump more sewage into them (or inexpertly leave lakes of it shimmering on the dump-station pavement), and every night the campground was filled to capacity.

The result was a stink that conquered it day by day—at night visibly, as a putrid mist, foggy miasma—until the campground was enveloped by the concentrated smell of human excrement. Nothing grew but the unimaginable stench. None could escape it, and all were complicit.

Staying indoors was the only recourse. The blast of air conditioners served, if not to remove, at least to mask the objectionableness. Outdoors, everybody breathed through the mouth in collective denial. Even the geese that summered at the ponds moved to the lake for the duration.

The heat wave that arrived with August baked the stench to an unbelievable intensification. It was a run three weeks long of 100+° days, five of which topped 110°. As Maureen's grandmother used to say, one day was hot and dry, the next dry and hot. Dennis continued to offer beer around the fire ring, but dispensed with the fire. Sunshine fell late into the evening with palpable weight.

One Saturday, he invited Rick and Jack to escape with him in a drive around the entire lake. He'd taken delivery of his new truck—a maroon four-door 4x4 long-bed diesel F-250, with a tawny leather interior and Bose sound system—only that morning.

Lady came along, too. They loaded her into the cargo bed and jammed themselves into the front seat. In honor of his fancy surroundings, Rick, in the middle, twisted forward to pull on a T-shirt. Jack yanked the tail down his back for him, flesh searing the heel of his hand. His penis immediately engorging, he casually pulled his own shirttail over his lap.

They waved at Sherry in the booth and, after a quick stop at QuikeeBuy for Dennis's smokes and to show off the truck, were off.

Poised importantly over the landscape, amidst upholstery and wood inlays more in the tradition of a British saloon car than an American pickup, they clipped west along the road that encircled the lake, past dried-up soybean fields and fresh-harvested wheat fields and Civil War historical markers. The countryside was a checkerboard tilted against the sky. There was traffic, but it was festive, high-summer-weekend traffic, largely trucks with kids stashed behind and pulling jet skis or boats.

It was good to be speeding along, great to get away from the smell.

They pulled off their road to visit a small lakeside park surrounding a half-drowned village whose blacksmith shop survived, a landmark of the Underground Railroad. That particular park featured grassy and aromatic bridle paths beneath the trees. They walked for a little, then sank to the edge of a trough. Rick visited ecstasies upon Lady while Dennis told them about Quantrill's massacre near by.

After a fitting silence, Dennis said, "Jack, been meaning to ask, coming back next year? I hope?"

"Don't think so, Dennis," Jack said. "Been great, I've enjoyed it, but next year I want to do something new. Not that I know what, yet."

"Yeah, cool," said Rick.

"Too bad," Dennis said. "Change your mind, let me know."

"You know, it's my first time working retail," Jack remarked, "and to meet people and not be able to *talk* is so strange. Some of them I'd like to know, some I think might like me, but we have to talk about permits—can't *connect*."

"That's about it," said Dennis.

"Though most seem blinded by the customer spotlight anyway. Maybe that's why we're a nation of shoppers? Addicted to our minute of stardom at the checkout?"

Rick laughed, but Dennis looked perplexed. Some riders coming up to water their horses, they relinquished the trough and drove into the sun.

They stopped next at the park that embraced the lake's western end. It devoted its grassy shoreline to tent camping, and they strolled it with pleasure. What was arid and stinking at Fort Horace was fresh and lovely there.

Finally, they turned south and east, eventually reaching a village of broad lawns, giant elms and upright old houses stately as any in New England. Sunlight skimming in at flat angles filled with yellow the huge vaults under the trees. Turning, they entered Oregon Bluff Park, Fort Horace's across-the-lake twin.

Parking at the marina, they sat watching the boats and looking across to Big Bone Hill. The lake's width did little to shrink the massif. They could make out their park's other landmarks, too: The swimming beach was a light-colored gash on the shoreline, and they could see cars nosing along Picnic Park Way.

As the blood-red sun bowled along the horizon, Lady walked them through a campground spread across slopes that went down to the water, through fields of tents and RVs, a veritable small town busy with cookouts, softball games, Frisbees flying, voices calling, kids running harmlessly wild. It was like happening upon a carnival in the open air. Nor was there any stench.

"Wonder if I should go meet the Vendor?" said Dennis, never veering. A little later, "Guys hungry?"

"Sure."

"Yeah."

"Pizza OK? My treat?"

"*Yeah!*"

"All *right!*"

Neon lettering splashed the hood as they pulled up in front of the village pizzeria. Inside they found pungent, enticing aromas, wooden booths and brick walls ornamented with antique scythes. Ordering a pitcher of Bud, they gravely discussed toppings, and ended up getting two large pies, with the expectation of having plenty to take home.

Every time Jack looked across, Rick's dark eyes were opening up at him out of a lean face favorably faceted with youth. He looked serious as well as handsome. A mole on his cheek exerted a fascination as Jack, looking into his eyes, unconsciously tried to keep it in focus.

"Rick, what are *your* plans?" he asked.

"Texas, I guess," said Rick. "Beanblossom's RV Park."

"What do you get out of that?"

"Three hots and a cot," he answered readily. "Oh, it's OK. They make me feel needed."

"Is that enough?"

"It'll do," Rick said. "For now."

"Why not move in with Lady and me? Seriously, you're welcome to."

"Long as he puts out, right?" said Dennis, clapping his mug on the table.

"That's exactly what I wouldn't ask him to do, *ever*," Jack replied. "There's plenty of room. You can have the double bunk in front—there's a curtain for privacy. Be the on-board mechanic and help drive. Lady's crazy about you. I'll feed you, you won't have to work. Probably going down to Florida this winter, but if you prefer Arizona or something, that's fine, too."

"Yeah, OK," said Rick, turning his face aside.

"Yeah?"

"Yeah, OK, I'll move in," Rick repeated.

"*Great*."

"But I don't want Sherry and Ernie to know yet. Hurt their feelings."

"My lips are sealed. Right, Dennis?"

"Sure," Dennis said. Jack saw his eyes narrow and his face clamp up as he suffered the blow.

They discovered they'd finished both pizzas. Jack insisted—*insisted*—on paying the check.

Darkness had fallen when they piled back into the truck and

woke up Lady with a crust. As they began to move Jack was startled to feel Rick's warm leg pressing his—definitely pressing. Very lightly, he pressed back. The young man's leg in the cab's intense cold burned his while Jack contemplated the possible return of love to his life. Or at least of sex, maybe. But closer to the park, as the tires hummed atop the dam, Rick shifted his leg away.

Then they were back amidst the stench. Dennis got his new smudge pots going—they helped a little—and gave them beers. Sherry was in the booth, while Ernie, as usual since the windfall, stayed indoors snug and smug in the glow of satellite.

Jack made a move. He slid down the bench, swung a leg around Rick's loins and, placing his hands on his shoulders, began to knead.

Rick arched his back and loosed grunts of relief. "Oh, *ma-an*," he gasped, "you've got the *touch*."

Jack eased backwards so his erection wouldn't trouble Rick.

Headlights X-rayed them. "Who's the wife and who's the husband?" jeered Percy.

Rick stood up fast and walked into darkness, leaving Jack with hands kneading air.

"I never know what people mean by that," he said.

"Oh, I think you do," Percy said. "Make a *lovely* couple." He raised his voice to taunt: "Still like *girls*, boy?" and drove off laughing.

Jack caught Dennis grinning into his beer.

## 22.

DURING THE GREAT STENCH, Rick usually took Bobby for a swim after a day's hauling. They piled shirtless into the van and snapped towels in the breeze all the way to the beach, not that it was far, a few hundred yards below Percy's Airstream.

And one Monday was so very hot—the mercury welded to 112°—that despite her general disinclination for sand and water, and self-conscious about fitting into a bathing suit, Maureen made a late-afternoon appearance.

But she was grateful, driving down beneath the trees, to leave the stench behind. At the beach she found perhaps two dozen people arranged on the soft tan sand.

Jack waved to her, and she spread her towel beside him. On his other side Rick lay supine in the sun with reptilian stillness, brown, smooth, but keeping an eye on Bobby in the water, too. Though trying not to feed on the sight of Rick, Jack nonetheless followed every breath swelling his tight belly as though it were a revelation.

Bobby meanwhile yelled about snapping turtles, made mock escapes from the water and finally prevailed on Rick to splash into it in his bright long trunks. Soon Rick was floating dreamily on the wavelets that lapped against the sand, powered less by tides than the unremitting *thump-thump-thump* of speedboats.

Across the cove Maureen saw Donna in a two-piece by herself, slathering her legs with lotion. She waved, but Donna didn't see, so, keeping her hair dry, she splashed across, emerging feeling buoyed up and cool.

"Hello, stranger!"

"Hi, Maureen."

"You're looking lovely."

"Thanks."

"Don't suppose I could bend your ear about an invitation to a certain wedding?"

Capping her tube, Donna looked up.

"Really want to be there, Maureen?"

"Oh Donna, *yes*. But I don't want to make trouble with your father."

Donna considered. "Leave it to me. Don't think I could go through it with without you, anyway."

Impulsively stooping to kiss her, Maureen smudged Donna with sand (she protested), fluttering inside, happy for the first time all summer.

She was still smiling that evening as she gave her white cat, Gerry, an airing in the middle of the loop. The sun finally losing ardor, a breeze sprang up and began pushing at the stench. The light was exquisite: It streamed horizontal, dispensing gold even as it searched and scoured.

Near by Jack held the leash while Lady ferreted out gopher dens. Gerry followed Lady at a remove. Her tail swinging deliberately, Lady widened select holes in sprays of dirt which, when she moved on, Jack discreetly shoed back into place. Meanwhile, Gerry sat himself down some ways off, looking aside, still and composed, eyes, ears and nose making minute adjustments.

When Lady, excited, pawed up a fountain of earth, Gerry pricked up his ears, studied the grass and pounced. He loped back towards Maureen's with a furry something in his mouth, though he dropped it and it scurried away. Lady was still digging.

"Like the moral to a Chinese fable: Dog labors, Cat reaps," Jack called. "Like a beer?"

"I'll bring my wine."

At Jack's picnic table a few minutes later, Lady's jaw was wedged in Maureen's lap, Maggie's in Jack's, both wriggling whenever petting was required.

"Big criminals," said Maureen as they touched coffee mugs. The light dug deep into their faces, setting age aside as it discovered their vitality. "So when's Rick moving in?"

"He'll let me know," Jack answered comfortably. He'd told her all about it. "One of these days, just do it. There's a funny angle, you know."

"Oh?"

"He's moving his stuff into the outside bins of Dennis's rig, at the rate of an item a day so the Beanblossoms don't catch on. And he who arrived without a shirt on his back now has the biggest wardrobe ever, every bit of it FREE. Could take years!"

"Are you in love with Rick?"

"Oh, no," he said instantly. "Who knows, though, if he weren't young enough to be my son?"

"Does age matter?"

"Not to me, of course."

"Haven't you noticed he's barely there? Blank, possibly blank all through? But with the most *reflective* surface? Like he's a mirror everyone sees himself in?"

"*Whoaa*, Maureen!"

"Well, and are we supposed to overlook his silly criminal record?"

"He seems an especially lost kid, waiting out a seven years' fate like someone in Greek mythology."

"Not merely an option-keeping-opener? And for any evidence to the contrary, not a bit bright, even if he does have an instinct for survival."

"And the bod to match. We'll see where it goes. Living together in a confined space? I have my hopes."

"I know you do, Jack, and I don't mean to offend, but I see you interested in Rick when all he does is tease."

"I know, I know," he sighed.

"Except you wonder how far he'll take it?"

"*Will tease for food* about covers it, I think."

"*Exactly:* As far as he needs to."

"But he's so beautiful," Jack pleaded.

"They're all skinny when they're young," scoffed Maureen, and voiced the fruit of her summer's meditation, released to say it by Donna's invitation, if with assistance from Chablis. "I'm worried you'll get hurt, Jack, but also I doubt it's *you*.

"You must have heard about my thing with Percy? At the time it seemed cost-free. But now I can see that to find in *Percy* the filling of a need was *cheap,* not who this little old lady really is. I wonder if Rick isn't your Percy?"

"Speaking of Percy," Jack said carefully. But she'd brought him up.

"Oh yes? Speaking of Percy?"

"Did you know he's been—won't say *stalking* me all summer, but that's what it amounts to?"

Her back straightened. "Surely not."

He told her about the drive-bys and flashlight patrols, the constant surveillance.

"Maureen, already it's so weird being gay, having everyone *terrified* of you while you just live your life and hope to meet someone you like—like anyone else, right? And then to have a *Percy* get after you— I mean, I assume in prison Percy had sex with men—"

"That's a *very* large assumption," Maureen declared. "Percy's *all* man, I assure you."

Jack let it go. He had anyway seen the Beanblossom van enter the loop and was wondering what it was up to, even as it turned in at his site and bounced over the grass to them.

Just back from the food bank with extra grapes and a pallet of avocados not quite rotten, tomatoes, corn and an emu egg, Eleanor Roosevelt was playing Lady Bountiful. At her window Jack accepted grapes and tomatoes, hefted but returned the emu egg, and offered beer. They declined, but Ernie, shirtless, turned off the engine as Sherry's mouth tightened. Something hung in the air.

Ernie ducked his head into the wash of sunlight to speak past Sherry.

"Hey, Jack?" he said, with such emotion that Jack cocked his head. The light probed Ernie also, his hair glinting metallically and his pallid naked chest with sunken nipples resembling a dry streambed. But the years dropped away, he was again a boy with fine features and vulnerable blue eyes. "So Rick's going with *you?*"

"Moving in, yeah," said Jack. "He told you?"

"Sherry guessed."

"He's been weird lately," Sherry said shortly. Her eyes were bulbs of resentment pinched against the sun.

"Kind of crowded with you all," Jack offered.

"Thirty-eight foot?" Sherry said scornfully. "Give me a fucking *break.*"

"Sherry," said Ernie. He looked devastated. "There goes Texas, I guess. He was going to help clear my land."

"Up to him."

"*I* think it's rotten," said Sherry. "Just so you know. Ernie won't say it."

"Sherry," Ernie repeated.

"You think you're better than us, Jack, that you're *exempt.* Go along, no responsibilities, *you'll* never get sick or starve. Leave that to the rest of us, thank you very much—leave *us* to find out on a daily basis how life is *shit.*"

"Sherry," Ernie said again, tenderly putting a hand across to her.

Seeing tears flood her eyes, and behind them a well of pure grief, Jack told her, "No, Sherry, I'm positively *not* exempt, not from *anything.* Even if apparently I want different things out of life than other people."

"Yeah, *right,*" she said, firmly handing back the emu egg.

She wiped her eyes and inhaled the mucous dangling from her nose as Ernie backed up the Astro and drove away. Jack called his thanks for the food, and stood doubtfully hefting the enormous egg.

"Well, I feel better," he told Maureen. "I *think*. Everything out in the open."

"Is it?" she answered. "I didn't realize they're *both* in love with Rick."

"Poor Sherry. The disorder of their lives doesn't bear thinking about."

"They'll move on soon," Maureen said. "Avert our eyes for us."

Jack watched the breeze brush the maples from green to silver, gilding them with a beautiful engraved quality. He realized as he stood cradling the emu egg in that ravishing light that the mass within was following his manipulations with a surprising substantiality.

"Hope Rick's not in for a bad night. Maureen, did you want this egg?"

## 23.

MAUREEN WOKE UP before dawn the next morning, definitively, with no possibility of falling back asleep. When you have cats, that sometimes will happen. But mostly it was excitement at being on Donna's guest list.

Night was just ebbing. She made coffee and, turning off the air conditioner, sipped it in the dark beside the open window. The stench was in partial pre-dawn remission, the smell insinuating itself inside the price of hearing the earliest-rising birds call. Her cats, having awakened her, chose to be scandalized by her getting up, but she winked at them and soon they were sleeping again.

From out of the night came the *thunk!* of a car bottoming out. Maureen saw no lights and heard no engine, only the unmistakable sound of a car's bottom hitting pavement. Which made no sense. The only hill a car could descend was Mark's driveway; there was no slope to the park road or to Apple Lane.

Then a vehicle drifted beneath the booth's streetlight from the direction of the ranger station; she had the impression of someone *pushing* it. Phantasmal shadows danced around it. As the lag of distance brought the sounds of trunk and doors being slammed shut, headlights went on—one did, anyway—and the car jerked away. A moment later, as it accelerated into the curve, came the sounds of its engine roaring to life and tires squealing.

*Kids*, she thought; kids from Fort Horace sneaking out after a night of sex and drinking at the boat ramps. Lucky the rangers didn't catch them.

Later, taking the mid-morning break prescribed by law, Percy munched a doughnut at the counter while paging through issues of *Guns & Ammo* and *Modern Bride*, in his mind's eye entertaining a vision of himself parading Donna across the top of Big Bone Hill to her bridegroom—to Mark standing there *terrified*, knees knocking, Adam's apple bobbing, the stuffing knocked out of him at last. *Sweet.*

Meanwhile a family arrived and tried the door, knocked, peered inside making helpful gestures, failed to understand the pinkie Percy directed to his *Back in 15 mins.* sign, knocked harder and looked disgusted. It made for a good show.

But a skinny kid in a ruffled yellow shirt who drove up and joined the family at the door failed to go with the program. He knocked and knocked and knocked.

Possibly because the kid's shirt matched Donna's uniform, Percy stepped to the door and pulled it open with an alarm of bells.

"What is it, son?"

"We were here first," a woman protested.
"Know where I can find Donna Bratcher, sir?"
"Who're *you*?"
"Sam! I work with her, Long John Silver's? She didn't show this morning, and her cell doesn't answer."
"Well, she's not here, is she?"
"You see her, sir, please tell her we need her."
"I'm her father, I'll take care of it."

The boy went on his way. Ignoring the others, Percy locked up and, groaning, climbed into his truck.

Ernie came over as he turned the key.

"Percy? Hey, Percy?"
"Make it snappy, Beanblossom."
"Ain't seen Rick, have you?"

Snorting, Percy spun his wheels on the gravel and made the turn up Mark's driveway. Mark's Corvette and official truck stood in the garage of his neat ranch house, but Donna's car was gone.

Percy rang and pounded. Finally Mark came out blinking sleepily.

"The fuck, Percy."
"Donna here?"
"She's at work," said Mark.
"No, she's not," said Percy, feeling a jolt of pure joy even as his features went rigid. "And that drifter character? Rick's gone, too."

Mark's face changed in an instant.

"Call Sheriff Jamie," he barked. "See if they're any warrants out on him."
"Did that long ago. He's clean."
"Then see if they're any out on *her*. *Do* it, Percy."

Mark turned and strode into the house, but Percy saw his face crumpling as he closed the door.

Percy's body arched in contempt. *Never get her now, motherfucker!* he proclaimed in mime, throwing a finger for good measure. His joy was overwhelming even though he suspected—*knew*—his job was toast. The last person Mark would want around now? A slave for life was facing freedom and the loss of everything he had.

Later Maureen went shopping at the Hy-Vee, where a voice called up the cereal aisle, "There's my harvest queen, more beautiful than ever!"

Maureen looked over to find a face she hadn't seen in 30-odd years, still wide-eyed and tremulous. Doug, her long-ago tongue-tied admirer, was, it turned out, divorced from the girl he married when Maureen wouldn't give him the time of day (it was complicated, she recalled: She was already going with Stan, so there was nothing personal in her rebuff) and newly retired to his hometown. His shyness appeared to have worn off.

She was delighted to see him—*delighted*—but found herself uncomfortable explaining that she lived in a trailer in the state park. But when he asked for it, she gave him her number.

When she got back to the park the temperature was over 100°. Unusually for a weekday, the Astro was home, Ernie standing near it. He waved her into his site. As she turned she saw a sheriff's car parked slantwise at the ranger station, as though intending a full-tilt departure.

"Hear about it?" Ernie asked.

"What's up, Ernie?"

"Rick and Donna. Took off together, looks like. From all indications."

The doors of Dennis's storage bins stood open on pistons, and she could see that they held only the tarps and wheel blocks they would have held before Rick began stuffing in his clothes.

Maureen realized she'd witnessed an elopement. That screaming rubber? She guessed the taunt of that screech—*So long, suckers!*—would prove the figure of Rick's and Donna's lives together, which would last however long it took to get wherever they were going plus a few weeks before he screeched off in her car without her. With luck neither leaving her pregnant nor a string of dead convenience-store clerks in his wake.

*Unless. . .* Unless somehow it worked out?

"SHE'S A SLUT," Sherry yelled out a window. "I COULD HAVE TOLD HIM."

"The way she breezed past the booth," Ernie said. "Butter wouldn't melt, my *ass*."

"SLUT. WHORE."

"Cunt," said Bobby as he came out the door.

"BOBBY, I WON'T STAND FOR THAT KIND OF LANGUAGE."

"But Mom, Rick's a *asshole*."

"Got that right," Ernie said. "Took him in, shared everything we have, and now *this*."

"ERNIE, TELL THEM TO DO AN AMBER ALERT."

Maureen told Ernie she was sorry and drove on. It gave her a lump in the belly, this futility in young lives. *What fools ye mortals be!* As she drove into the loop she saw Jack reading at his picnic table, Lady folded in the shade at his feet. She knew she was elected, so pulled in.

He came over to her window.

"Hey, Maureen, know what I've been watching?" he said. "Crows wiping out a family of sparrows in that tree. They get a fledgling, it screams and the poor brave parents dart at them. Nest's empty now."

"Birds are cruel, but their lives are hard," she said. "Jack, Rick's gone. Rick and Donna both, last night." Looking away from the hurt in his eyes, she added, "I'm sorry," and went inside her trailer.

## 24.

DENNIS'S FIRE RING the night after Donna and Rick decamped (Maureen and Jack agreed on the *mot juste*) was a wake. Thoughts and hearts were with the one-eyed Isuzu chewing up the miles, the hood bouncing against its bungee cord en route to wherever.

Interstate 70 was grumbling. A truck would push something throaty and diesel up the scale until like death in miniature it would decrescendo and drop away. Occasionally came the coughing of jake brakes.

From the booth Rupert, the retired farmer, oversaw a steady flow of vehicles. Rupert had worked booth for years. Whenever on his shift people whisked in saying they "just wanted" to do this or "just needed" to do that—implying that it was absurd *they* be required to pay admission—Rupert repeated "Five dollars" until they paid up or turned around. Maureen didn't know him well. She thought she could detect a dry sense of humor.

Ernie hummed *Drifter* at a suitably funereal pace, and mourned, "Rick would have loved Texas. *Loved* it."

"He's a asshole," Bobby reminded him. Bobby was doubly bereft, for while putting Diego in his kennel that afternoon the dog slipped his chain and ran into the woods, not to be seen again.

"So young," said Dennis.

"Glad I'm not," Jack put in. At his feet Lady looked disheveled by the general disturbance.

"Hope that beater gets 'em where they're going," said Ernie, giving a vivid pink view of gums. "Only thing holding it together's Kentucky chrome."

"*Kentucky chrome?*" asked Jack.

Ernie spat. "What you call duct tape."

Solemnly, Sherry said, "Know I saw his little tushy?"

"Really?" said Dennis.

"*Twice,*" she sighed.

"Wonder how Percy's taking it?" Jack asked.

"*Not* the day to ask where the crappies are biting," sniffed Sherry.

"Well, his job's good as gone," declared Jack, trying not to gloat.

"Percy might be *glad* Mark's not marrying her," Maureen said. "Makes him less dependent, which, according to *The Code of the Bratchers*, is what a man ought to be."

"You should know," Sherry said serenely.

Ernie got out-and-out drunk; probably Dennis too, though no one could tell for sure. It was a festival of self-pity. The night before, no one knew Rick was anything but a spectator of his own life, Donna anything but a blushing bride; the night after, their flight looked inevitable, though no one expressed sympathy for her or *her* dilemma.

Percy loomed up in the dark, unseen until he sat himself down with a groan. He was drunk, too.

"Dennis, s'not *beer* I see, is it?"

"Busted," said Dennis.

"Serious, don' wanna get kicked out. You know the rules." That got everyone going. The cans vanished into Dennis's. "More like it."

Percy scrutinized Maureen as he never did when sober.

"How are you, Percy?" she asked.

"How you *think* I am?"

"How's Mark holding up?"

"He'll live, thanks ver' much, though he don't think so." Percy smirked. "They're in California, I'm thinking, or headed there, and no laws broken."

"Isn't a headlight out?" Jack asked. "Put out an APB."

A vein throbbed in Percy's neck. "Didn't put the move on him, they'd still be here," he informed Jack. "Saw you rubbing him."

"People do what they want, Percy."

"Treat him like a faggot, what's he s'posed to do? No *wonder* he ran. Me, I'm Wile E. Coyote treading air, 'cause I just went off the fucking *cliff*. Mark's on me like you wouldn't believe."

"Oh, surely not," said Maureen.

"Sat me down, hinted times are changing, got to adapt. Adapt myself right on out of *here,* he means. Why keep me on *now?* To remind him of *Donna?* Fire me sure, soon's he finds the nerve."

"Don't say that," Maureen said. She had a scary feeling that Donna's removal from the scene—whatever it might mean for Mark—deprived Percy of his sole hostage to life, meant he was free of control, could slip *his* chain.

"Say anything I goddam well please." And even Percy seemed about to break. "Whole wedding planned and paid for? Well, shit on that, I guess. Donna don't want it, *must* be shit. Got the permit for Big Bone Hill, shelter 'A' for the day—*with* power. Cake on order—buttercreme, the *works*. The goddam dress, goddam *Travis,* even a fucking *band*. So fuck *her*. *Fuck* Donna and *fuck* her fucking *mother.* . . Hell, got one for me?"

Dennis retrieved a can of beer, and Percy upended it, drank it down, crushed it in his fist and held it out for another.

Charged with an idea, Sherry was quivering immensely.

"She'll be sorry, Percy," she assured him in her most cultivated manner. "Real sorry, *real* soon. God, I'm so envious of what she just threw away: Ernie and me'll get hitched by some clerk somewhere, and your girl had it *all.*"

Percy looked over, his reaction slowed by liquor, and Sherry had to shush whatever it was Ernie got it in his head to suggest.

"Well, know what, since s'all shet?" Percy said, sinking a hand in her knee. "Let me give you lovebirds a present: Donna's wedding, Labor Day Shaturday. Be there or be square."

"Thank you, Percy," said Sherry instantly. "That's so fucking generous of you! Oh, I'm going to cry. Hear that, Ernie? We're getting *married.*"

"Percy, you can't give Donna's wedding away!" Maureen said.

"Don't cheapen it!"

Percy looked pleased with himself as he peeped at the moon.

"Hey man, thanks a lot," said Ernie, inspired to brevity. "Hope you'll be my best man?"

"Nah, but ask Mark, why don't you? He's free that day."

A sudden thought struck Sherry. "Ohmigod, will her dress *fit?*"

Percy threw back his head and brayed laughter. From not far away a pack of coyotes answered.

## 25.

A STEADY NEW BREEZE blew the stench away the next day and moderated the temperature.

The heat wave was over, but its work was done. It was as though grass fires had swept the region, leaving behind a sere, brown, cracklingly dry landscape. Grasses had withered to the ground, become so much matted straw. The very trees were limp and dull. Only the sunflowers still made a stand with stretched necks and bright lolling faces.

The ache of Rick's flight lingered, and no one acted it out so directly as Bobby. Dennis handed him his opportunity when he gave him ten bucks to roll an old Toro around his site. The mowers were busy with other duties, but Dennis watered every day and his lawn was getting shaggy.

Bobby did the job while Dennis was at work. He had fun with it! In the long growth beside the road he wrote in green the word he wished to thrust in the world's face, by dint of starting and stopping the lawnmower carving out a giant

# FUK

"So much for home-schooling," Jack remarked that evening.

Bobby also managed to sever the cable leading to the satellite dish. Loud were the lamentations, frequent the invocations of his word, for the period when the Beanblossoms could foregather in front of their fancy TV was—just like that—over; the satellite-dish people for reasons best known to themselves declined to fix it, and the Beanblossoms were back at the fire ring. Meanwhile Dennis mowed his grass to inoffensiveness himself.

It seemed to Jack, in light of the Rick debacle—taking a tentative step towards waking up his heart, only to have the rug pulled out from under him, however deservedly—the responsible, adult thing to do was to have an adventure in the Picnic Park. He was human, male, gay, with needs only cock could fulfill. High time he lost certain illusions, certain hopes, and acceded to middle age's more comradely, more cosmic view, which jettisons the cock particular—apt to be difficult to get, possibly treacherous to boot—in favor of the cock universal.

That Saturday evening, he rode his Trek into the Picnic Park at 7:00 o'clock.

To his dismay it was at peak activity. Every pavilion sheltered an affair, even the surviving platform at the tornado-smashed one. It was aggravating, if charming, to see the picnic rites enacted: the relaxed and pleasant air, the women coalescing and splitting apart, the men ganging together and, off by themselves, the teenagers, grimfaced to adult observation but lively amongst themselves, and in the event not straying far from the barbecue. Even the gazebo was hosting a veterans gathering.

To pass the time he left the park, setting out across the dam and meandering along the country lanes of the old river valley, never losing the incongruous sound of speedboats *thump-thump-thumping* across the Kansas plains.

Finally he turned around and glided back into the Picnic Park. It was nearly 9:00 p.m. and, though the sun was fast losing buoyancy, still light. The pavilions were now either abandoned or being cleaned up. Despite quaffing from his water bottle, Jack felt dry as he rounded the curve that would disclose the gazebo: It was H-Hour of D-Day.

There was no one there.

He figured he might as well set up shop, see what developed. If nothing else, it was a pleasant place to pass a lovely evening. The WPA had sited the pavilions atop bluffs rising over what was then the river. The failing light every moment altered the lake's appearance.

At the first moment of real darkness—modified by the popping on of a streetlight over the gazebo's parking spaces—a car came up, paused where Jack's bike leaned against a tree, passed onward and turned in at the next pavilion, the tornado-smashed one. Someone got out and made his way back.

Jack, his heart thumping, could see little until the man braved the streetlight's cone. It revealed a fine figure in shorts and T-shirt smoking a cigarette and directing a dirty look at Jack's shadows. Jack apprehended that dirty looks were part of the play action, serving to relieve both parties from being themselves, thus contributing to lubricity. He glared back but doubted he could be seen. The man stood sentry until he flicked the butt away; Jack hoped the cigarette signaled an oral need.

Stepping under the roof, the man came up close to challenge, in a low voice, "Are you a cop?"

"No," murmured Jack. "Are you?"

"No," breathed the man, and touched him. "Are you married?"

"No."

"I am," the man whispered and, endearments done, they proceeded.

Soon as though it pained them they were gushing sweetness down each other's throats.

"*Nice,*" the man said when he ceased to tremble. They held each other. "Thanks."

"Thank *you,*" Jack replied.

"See you again, I hope," the man said. He returned to his car and drove away.

Jack mounted his bike, lighted headlight and taillight, and rode home. His mouth felt kissed all over, his body in a state of grace for the first time in too long.

It occurred to him that never before had he shared joyful sex with someone whose name he didn't know. *Welcome to the human race!*

## 26.

AS DAY CLOSED, Percy liked to sit outside his trailer and feed the squirrels. He was trying to tame one who took his fancy by reason of its bare tail, and hoped it would take the place of the late Rocky. But Shooter, wary of his overtures, was making the courtship an extended one.

The Airstream afforded Percy a view back along the woods track to it and then across 100 yards of meadow clear to a stretch of Picnic Park Way below the Osage chief. Even when the trees were in leaf, he could, if he cared to, monitor traffic in and out of the Picnic Park.

Sometimes he saw Jack bike into the Picnic Park and come out in just the time it took to pedal the loop. But one evening while teasing Shooter with pecans, he saw Jack *twice* ride into the Picnic Park, first at its peak time—he didn't linger—and then at dusk. Some time passed before the lights of a bicycle left again.

Percy perked up. He knew what Jack was up to!

Over the course of the next few weeks several times again towards sunset he noticed Jack biking into the Picnic Park and pedaling out long enough later that he had to have been up to something.

He consulted Ranger Ray about how to fix him once and for all, and they devised a plan. Jack wouldn't even know whom he was servicing until he was placed under arrest, a revelation that would *destroy* him! Oh, the look on his face!

Plans in place, Percy was sitting outdoors feeding Shooter one sweet evening, the park astir with the sounds of a summer day drawing towards its close. Residents visited one another in their rough-running trucks, visitors were busy at the grills, kids laughing, boats returning to the marina *putt-putt-putt*.

Maureen was working booth.

"Late for a ride, isn't it?" she asked Jack as he paused on his way out.

"But so pretty," he told her. "And I have my lights."

Minutes later, Percy's truck emerged from the woods, passed the booth without the customary toot of the horn, and turned into the Picnic Park. Then Ranger Ray drove past, slow and easy, waving at Maureen, and he also entered the Picnic Park.

At the gazebo Jack found himself alone in the dark. The only light in the sky was lividity towards Fort Horace. But he felt some disquiet, too, and stood still to analyze it. He realized the streetlight was out.

At the next pavilion a car's interior light winked on and a door slammed. Jack could discern a man coming closer with a rolling gait. His heart sank as he perceived him to be fat and old; older than himself, at any rate.

Soon he was making the acquaintance of Daryll, chatty historian of the gazebo's years as a trysting place. Unfazed by Jack's lack of interest in him, Daryll spoke nostalgically of the orgies of yore—the Seventies, particularly, lived on in memory. He attributed to the inroads of the Internet the somewhat chilly present-day pace of activity.

Daryll was curious about Jack's Picnic Park encounters and pressed for details. Jack complied, but the telling brought him up short. How far he was from how he'd looked at sex his whole life, as not an end in itself but an expression of intimacy. One night he'd gobbled the organ of a man who watched with seeming contempt. Another night *he* remorselessly made a guy gag. On another occasion, he was bringing it out when his prospective partner said, "I can't do this," and fled.

His first encounter had filled him with grace, but the episodes since lacked any shared tenderness. So what the hell was he doing?

"Slow night," said Daryll.

They heard an engine approach. A vehicle wreathed in darkness breezed up and stopped. A door opened and closed with no light showing, and steps crunched on gravel. Obeying instinct, Jack blurted, "I'm out of here, Daryll," and melted to the trees. He came around to the road to find Percy's pickup parked next to his bicycle. He lifted the bike, locking the wheels to prevent any penetrating metallic sound—any sound at all—and carried it down the road. Past the next curve he mounted and rode home.

Meanwhile Percy stepped into the gazebo. He had the advantage, having disconnected the streetlight himself. He could just make out someone: *Jack*. Had he not seen Jack enter the Picnic Park, and was that not Jack's bike beside his truck? Had to be *Jack* waiting to service whatever flesh happened to come along, with no idea it would be *his*. Had to be *Jack* who now was duly scrabbling at his crotch, unbuttoning his jeans and taking him in his mouth.

"Suck it," murmured Percy.

## THE WEDDING ON BIG BONE HILL

The sensations visited upon him, though purely incidental to his performance of a semi-official function, were enjoyable nonetheless. Unintentionally, as lips worried his cock as a cat does its prey, he uttered vulnerable cries of gladness and freedom, almost sobbed. And despite heroic resistance—for legal purposes it was best not to go so far, though resistance also served to extend and heighten his pleasure—he came with mighty groans and spasms. The lips were smacking when Percy—keeping one hand tight on the other's head—touched the walkie-talkie at his belt to summon Ranger Ray, then, gasping, "Gotcha now, *faggot*," switched on his flashlight and found himself looking at Daryll's gratified face.

He was startled and dismayed. Naturally he wished to leave Daryll with a souvenir, but Daryll hadn't spent a lifetime being gay-bashed without picking up some useful moves, and so while Daryll slipped untouched out of the Picnic Park, Percy's eye was beginning to pass through the colors of the rainbow.

When Ranger Ray pulled up in a spray of gravel shouting, *"What've we got, Percy?"* Percy just said, "Sorry, false alarm."

Ray looked at him and almost said something—heaving and out of breath, Percy kept his left side turned away—but thought better of it and drove off. Percy hurried home and microwaved a frozen steak to a sloppy approximation of room temperature and slapped it on.

In the meantime Jack told Maureen he'd had a lovely ride.

He didn't mention that riding home he'd made a decision: To renounce the Picnic Park, renounce going to the gazebo to await events or meet whoever was there. It wasn't that his close call with Percy scared him—though it did—but in the end the stray excitement, the fugitive human contact he found there wasn't enough. Randomness didn't serve, sexually speaking.

*Let's keep it personal,* he told himself. *At least personal. However infrequent, what sex I have will be personal.*

## 27.

THOUGH ABSORBED IN every detail of preparations for her big day, Sherry was especially attentive to the alterations to Donna's wedding dress.

That triumph of Viola's Bridal Shoppe obsessed her. She couldn't pull it on however she wriggled, could do no more than bunch it at her neck or hold it to her front. But in the event, a park wife Maureen recommended, a former seamstress, forthrightly cut off the train and found in it yardage enough to wrap Sherry's torso, if somewhat in the manner of a sausage casing.

Sherry let it be known she wanted a bridal shower. But nobody threw one. When it came down to it, Maureen had no stomach for such a travesty, and no one else did, either. Nor did Ernie get a bachelor's party.

However, Maureen did go in with Dennis and Jack on the gift of a fine gas grill. It seemed to go over, give added luster to eyes on the lookout for anything FREE.

And against her better judgment, she consented to stand up with Dennis for the bride and groom. They were grateful, except that Ernie reverted to gloom whenever he remembered that Rick was to have been his best man.

"Said he would, but—" he said, beating back tears. "But *anyway*."

A rehearsal there was no avoiding. It was set for Friday before sunset, 24 hours before the wedding. Since Friday of Labor Day weekend was the booth's busiest day of the year—and Saturday the second-busiest—Dennis faced a scheduling problem, which he solved by assigning Jack and Rupert to team up both days and paying them minimum wage.

That morning, looking ahead to the happy event, Maureen had lain abed, taking stock. An elopement by two young people who knew what they wanted? Followed by this burlesque of a wedding? It somehow seemed a wake-up call.

She'd had her time at the park, she concluded. Her mourning—whether for her husband, or for marrying the wrong man in the first place, or possibly just for her youth—was quite finished, as was her thing with Percy. She'd met Doug again, too; whatever might happen, that there *were* Dougs in the world was something to bear in mind.

Now it was time to move on—time to plug the box of wine, hitch up the trailer. So she was past 50? She had good years left, the *best*, if only she got her act together. Not that she'd ever look down on people who live in trailers, but some nice houses were for sale in Fort Horace. She was attracted less by the piles of grandeur in her old neighborhood than by new condos above the river, with gardens and a view, sufficient but not superfluous space, within walking distance of everything, if away from the park and its denizens trying to work out their destinies.

Dennis walked with Maureen up to the rehearsal. Big Bone Hill's prairie grasses had shriveled, although sunflowers still swayed over the rich reds and browns, but the turf pathway (which Travis promised to mow in the morning) held a memory of green. The lake made silver slashes in a landscape that at every point of the compass barns and silos composed into picturesqueness. They could see vehicles pouring into the park.

Climbing Big Bone, Maureen was in a funny mood, the mood of someone doing something maybe for the last time.

Percy and Travis (who for once wore a suit, stuffing it like a scarecrow) awaited them, along with Sherry and Ernie, she in pink sweats, he in cutoffs and wife-beater ("But what did we expect?" Maureen whispered to Dennis).

The intendeds held hands until Travis parted them, brought Ernie up and instructed Percy (who couldn't resist personally giving the bride away) to escort Sherry forward. He did so in high glee, telegraphing mockery with his twitching upper lip; Maureen sensed disorder and tumult straining to get out of him. Yellow still framed his left eye; the discoloration lasted longer than belief in his story about surprising an unlicensed night fisherman who threw a floodlight at him, and somehow lent credence to the rumor he was about to be fired.

Travis was nervous, as Maureen thought befitted a mail-order minister, but solemn and respectful, too. He knew the script and helped the bridal couple learn their lines. Altogether, she conceded, he lent gravitas to the affair.

For Ernie and Sherry she actually felt hope after seeing the look they exchanged, rosy sunlight washing their features clear of acquisitiveness, and she began to shed tears.

Afterwards everybody repaired to Maureen's site for dinner. It was the least she could do, she thought, to make potato salad and grill cheeseburgers for the happy couple. Dennis supplied the beer. Travis didn't linger; he didn't drink and seeing anyone do so sorrowed him, but Percy tolerantly helped wrestle over an extra picnic table.

Watching Percy eat, Maureen thought she noticed a new mannerism, an occasional spontaneous opening of his left hand, fingers blossoming in acquiescence or greeting—something, it struck her, to do with Fate. She wondered if Mark really was going to fire him.

She chose her moment to say, "Travis was a good choice, Percy. You were right and I was wrong."

Percy belched, and soon got up and drove home.

Ernie started chugging his brewskis, belching grandly, and

— *THE WEDDING ON BIG BONE HILL* —

Sherry accepted several thimblefuls. Mark dropped by to express from his Corvette a gracious wish for the Beanblossoms' happiness, showing as deft a touch for ignoring beer in front of his face as any ranger.

Talk drifted to the future. The U.S. Government had thoughtlessly lobbed the bride a stink bomb that very day: A letter from SSI demanded the return of her dowry, claiming the $5,000 payment to have been made in error. If she didn't return it immediately — and of course it was long gone — her monthly check would be withheld until the accumulated total made up the larger sum. It would take more than half a year.

"Sherry, why not get a job and stay the winter?" Maureen suggested, forbearing any *I-told-you-so*. "The Hy-Vee always needs cashiers. You could put Bobby in school, save money and be comfortable off the road for awhile."

"Trouble is," Ernie answered for Sherry, "we got a dream of Texas, don't we, babe?"

"Not to mention a real opportunity to test Jesus," Sherry said evenly.

Maureen dished up peach ice-cream for dessert, satisfied that her dinner was a success.

Suddenly, horns blaring, a club van and a station wagon rolled onto her grass. It was Ernie's brother, uncle, three cousins, two friends and a guy picked up along the way arriving with two kegs of beer after a nonstop drive from Indiana.

In horror Maureen forbade setting up the kegs on her picnic table. They stayed in the back of the van instead, and soon the newcomers and the Beanblossoms were beerily reminiscing while scarfing up the last of dinner and dessert.

They hadn't seen Ernie, everyone agreed, since the big fight at his mother's wake three years earlier. *That* had been a time! Standing beside the open casket, Ernie insisted he only wanted fairness, but Mama's dresses being *way* too small for Sherry, they deserved the *truck*. His brother disagreed. Everybody laughed now: The engine blew not 1,000 miles later! But at the time words were exchanged, sides taken, shoves given and received, with the unfortunate result that the trestles holding up the casket collapsed and Mama flopped out onto the floor.

"And no *shoes!*" wailed Sherry.

"Fucking *barefoot*," said Ernie, "even though we gave them her second-best pair. Better believe I got in their face about that!"

"All we could do to get her planted next day," Uncle remembered, "but we did it. She's in the ground today."

Ernie's relatives got themselves refills and as naturally as another family might collect the forks or put the lids back on the pickle jars took out their assault rifles and asked who had the targets.

But a concerted honking from the booth's direction interrupted.

"They're here, Ernie!" said Sherry, and screamed, "OVER HERE, YOU FAT BROADS!"

It was met with 50 iterations of "Woo-*hoo!*"

"Orgy time, guys!" Ernie announced. "Anyone can't get laid *tonight—!*"

The cars, Sherry explained, carried honorary bridesmaids and groomsmen summoned via the Web—friends from a national organization called *Frankly Fat Femmes d'Allure* devoted to big women and those who admire them.

"Booked for the Scout Camp," she said. The Scout Camp was a meadow above the boat ramps set aside for group tent camping. "Let's show 'em the way, Ernie."

Their contingent scrambled off and soon was heading a cavalcade up the road.

Dennis helped Maureen clean up. Jack biked over, released by Rupert when the rush finally slowed. After retrieving Lady from his rig, he gratefully joined in roasting marshmallows for S'Mores. Overhead, redfaced Mars glowered at Diana from a markedly greater distance than earlier that summer.

There was the sound of a rifle shot. Maggie and Lady flinched, and were put indoors crying.

Atop Big Bone, Maureen had noticed the air losing its summertime heft, sound becoming more resonant, more apt to travel. Now it weightlessly carried the burp of automatic rifle fire and a woman's scream, both coming from the direction of the Scout Camp. More shots, more screams followed.

She went indoors to radio the rangers, but none immediately responded, so she phoned the Sheriff's Department. Flight upon flight of rifle fire brought visitors and residents outside their rigs, some bearing their own guns.

The screams continued, too. On the radio Maureen heard Travis get through to Ranger Randy about terrorists, and Randy's truck hurtled up the road, siren wailing and lights flashing. Percy was right behind, delayed on the trip from the Airstream, the radio said, only by the time it took to stop and grab the ranger station's shotgun.

When the police arrived, it was in force, Sheriff Jamie in person with Mark sitting beside him and two sheriff's cars following, plus three Fort Horace patrol cars, two State Police units pulled off I-70 and an ambulance.

Screams meanwhile rang out continuously from the bluffs. Cocking her head, Maureen ventured to guess that, actually, they sounded like screams of pleasure.

"Rape of the Sabine Women," Jack agreed, adding, "not that that's p.c."

Eventually the shooting stopped, the screams quieted down and law enforcement reappeared, the sheriff leading a caravan headed by the club van and station wagon out of the park.

Percy's truck brought up the rear, turning into the loop and stopping at Maureen's. Mark spoke from the passenger seat in a shaking voice.

"Listen up, Dennis: Told your freakin' hillbillies that unless they want their relatives held for trial, they and their freakin' *motorhome* and all their effin' *stuff* better be *out* of my park noontime *tomorrow*."

"But the wedding—"

"Wedding's *off*," Mark snarled, Percy sneering behind him. "Won't *be* any fucking wedding."

Gravel showered the ground behind as the truck drove off.

The moon set and the Milky Way powdered itself across the sky. Maureen and Dennis and Jack, wanting to stretch out the moment, which felt like the last moment of summer, sat on while the fire in the grill crackled down to coals. Restored to the peaceful outdoors, Lady and Maggie slept jammed up against each other.

Despite the police action, the Scout Camp resounded with cries of ecstasy all night long.

## 28.

NO ONE THOUGHT to tell Travis the wedding was off, though perhaps he should have gathered the fact from the radio traffic, or else seen Ernie and Sherry in the morning.

Hung over, with no good grace they flung things into their motorhome (but leaving the vast majority of their riches littering acres, the mess reading as an anguished cry: If *stuff* can't save us, what *will?*). Finally, after borrowing gas money from Dennis, the Beanblossoms pulled out in their land yacht stonily refusing to say a word of farewell.

It was the talk of the park, after all. But later everyone agreed it was possible that, having said he would mow the path up Big Bone, Travis simply wanted to go ahead and do it.

Driving his tractor to the hill's base, he zigged and zagged upward, leaving a perfect ribbon of close-cropped, even turf—a pretty piece of mowing. At the top, as events were reconstructed, he must have seen a rattlesnake; although no one mentioned it to the bride or groom, Big Bone Hill was notorious for them.

Travis must have leapt off the tractor with his machete and pursued the rattler over the matted grass towards Apple Lane. Stepping in a hole, he grievously gashed his thigh. The rattlesnakes whose den it was struck his leg over and over again.

Somehow he got back to the Deere, but it careered straight downhill over the native grasses and at the road turned not towards his site but inexplicably chugged the other way, accumulating a tail of cars that honked with the *Listen to this!* insistence of a bridal procession.

As Travis passed the booth—his gaze distant, preoccupied—Jack and Rupert were too caught up with inbound traffic to guess the meaning of the spectacle across the divider. Of course, they couldn't see the blood trail he was leaving.

At the curve he apparently lost consciousness; his loosened grip sent tractor and blades careening into the gully. Everything that could be done was done with the freneticism that attends modern-day death. Racing against the most certain event known, even a medevac helicopter was brought in so as to jump the traffic.

But poor Travis was well and truly gone.

## 29.

TRAVIS'S DEATH shocked the park, but the long weekend wore on.

Sunday was another perfect day. The park was packed, every site occupied, every parking space filled. *Thump-thump-thump* came continuously from the water. The beach crawled with swimmers. Pickup football teams ran roughshod over meadows. People pushed up to TVs on the sides of motorhomes to watch baseball and NASCAR, yelling savagely.

In late afternoon the radio carried word of another tragedy, off Oregon Bluff across the lake, the sort of grotesque thing that seems to happen every Labor Day weekend: A youth losing control of his jet ski, it crossed the deck of a speedboat at anchor and beheaded a woman sipping white wine.

Maureen was supposed to have dinner with her long-lost friend. She called to cancel, explaining she thought staying home would honor Travis. But it sounded stupid, hearing herself say it, and she relented. Doug picked her up so he could meet her animals.

And by some miracle, they seemed to start again where they'd left off senior year. Memory, she realized, makes time a comforter that can fold today next to long ago. She liked the way Doug's eyes returned to her after she presented Maggie; you don't look at what you don't want to. Dinner was a pleasure.

Monday dawned overcast and cool, as though summer were over, done with, *finished*.

The park always hosted two mountain-bike races on Labor Day, one a 10k, the other 25k. Both courses, though starting and ending on the road, mostly followed trails through the woods. All morning vehicles finned with bicycles thronged into the park. From the booth Maureen and Rupert waved them into the meadow that reached towards the lake between Percy's Airstream and the Picnic

Park, where Jack helped Dennis collect fees and direct cars into rows. Meanwhile, by permission, Lady hung out in the booth.

One cyclist, to Jack adorable in Spandex, was his married man from the gazebo. Jack said warmly, "Hi, how are you?" and the other hooded his eyes and lifted his bike off his roof without responding. His cute male companion gave Jack a sharp look.

Packs of cyclists began warming up. Personally overseeing the races from his Cannondale, Mark walkie-talkied the booth to order a halt to traffic, and Rupert duly dragged sawhorses across the lanes. The cannon sounded, the pack rushed down the road and vanished into the woods. Mark radioing again, Rupert pulled the sawhorses out of the way.

They closed the road once more when the pack came back to it, and an hour later repeated their actions for the other race.

Both races run and medals awarded, most of the cyclists hoisted their bikes aboard their vehicles and left, though others stayed on to ride the trails as Labor Day continued to unfold in its traditional unstudied way. The sun was warm, but the shade remained cool. Smoke from grilling meat drifted across the park. At the ranger station Percy mediated between the driver of an Expedition and the owner of the trailer-mounted sailboat it collided with. Their mutual rage was a tonic to him.

Dennis released Jack from parking duty, and he collected Lady for a walk before his final booth shift of the weekend. After briefly razzing Maureen and Rupert on how busy they were, he followed Lady towards the beach.

Some time later, in an unruffled voice Ranger Ray alerted "all stations" to the fact of a missing boy: nine years old; four feet, four inches tall; 75 pounds; blond; blue eyed; Spiderman cycling outfit and helmet; last seen riding a kid-size mountain bike with his parents and sister on a trail near the beach. After turning around to find their boy *gone*, the parents had flagged down Ray, who added that they were "rather hysterical."

Within seconds Percy was out of the ranger station and launching his truck.

He braked at the booth. "Maureen, where's *Jack?*"

Reading *"Finally!"* in his eyes, she saw the sawed-off shotgun on the seat beside him.

"He was helping Dennis park cars," she replied. Dennis was lounging against one of the last vehicles left in the meadow, counting chunks of money and stuffing his pockets. "Now he's walking his dog."

*"Where?"*

She told him. Had to. Disgust glazing his features, he turned on his siren and sped off towards the beach like an avenging angel. She heard him radio Ranger Ray that *Jack* was reported to be in the missing boy's vicinity, they might have themselves a *situation*.

"Ten-four," replied Ray. "Who's manning the station?"

Percy didn't reply, so Maureen put in, "No one, I think, 71, but I'll call Mark."

She speed-dialed and filled him in. Mark told her he'd be there within two minutes, and she relayed the news even as he came into sight pedaling standing up on his Cannondale for greater speed.

As soon as Mark went indoors he came on the radio to say, "Twenty-five to all stations: Sheriff's on the way. 54, hold traffic till further notice."

"Ten-four, 25," Maureen answered, and Rupert dragged the sawhorses into the lanes, unfolded the plastic wrap from his sandwich and began to eat.

Mark came back on to say, "Twenty-five to 31, 25 to 31, come in." Impatiently: "Percy, are you there? Percy, will you please *say* something?"

Moments later a sheriff's car stormed into the park on the unblocked exit lane, the first of a panoply of cars to converge, some of them the grays and browns that proclaim undercover vehicles. Most, sirens wailing discordantly, were directed to the beach.

Someone on the radio was compiling descriptions of the boy and Jack in preparation for an Amber Alert when somebody broke in to report that an Arab-looking man had just been seen buying a soda at Showerhouse B's machine.

Cars dashed off there, and reports followed about crouching cops, weapons drawn, making the visitor drop his Mountain Dew and his pants, raise his hands and lie face down on the ground. After they searched him and his car, they took him to the ranger station and sat him beside Mark's desk, no longer worried that he'd abducted the boy, but on general principles not letting him go yet, either.

Incoming traffic stacked up around the curve beyond the Osage chieftain. Honking horns filled the octaves between sirens; the noise skinned Maureen's nerves.

From the booth she scanned the woods in search of the little boy, and happened actually to see Jack break into the meadow at a run. She wondered if he knew that at that distance khaki shorts made him look nude. Lady was gamboling about him at leash's end, but Maureen apprehended that Jack was running for his life even before she saw Percy's truck smash out of the trees behind him. It bounced and jounced across the meadow; she could hear the engine laboring. It caught up to Jack, but Jack darted towards the water. Percy leapt out to give chase. Jack was more fleet of foot, but Percy had the gun.

Fate is tone deaf, it persists in unfolding in ironic monotone.

The radio heralded the glad news that the little boy lost was found. Turned out that without ever realizing he was missing, he rode from the side path he'd blundered onto back into the midst of his searchers and was reunited with his father. They were en route to the ranger station.

Maureen meanwhile saw Percy capture Jack. Jack turned around and put up his hands, his right hand part way because of the leash. Percy marched man and dog to his truck, had Jack load

Lady in its bed, then forced him behind the wheel. Meanwhile sirens were made to whoop with joy, and the triumphal procession bearing the boy emerged from the beach road.

Percy's truck began bouncing towards the road, Lady sliding around the rear, and his voice came on the radio.

"Thirty-one to 25, come in."

Maureen could hear his pleasure, the satisfaction of a job well done.

"This is 25," said Mark. "Percy, what the *h-e-double-hockey-sticks* is going on? And where's my effin' shotgun?"

"Sorry, but I needed it," said Percy. "Bringing your faggot in now."

"Thirty-one, you mean *Jack*? He's clean, let him go."

"Little boy missing? I will *not*—"

"Thirty-one, boy's been found. Repeat, little boy's OK. Safe and sound, on his way up here now."

Percy took a moment to respond. "Where was he, 25?"

"Pine grove, west of the beach."

Which Maureen—Percy even better—knew was a good half-mile as the crow flies from where he accosted Jack, farther via the paths.

"Hell, Mark, I saw Jack grab the kid! He was pulling down his *pants*, kid was *screaming*! Miracle I got there when I did!"

That's what Percy said. No one responded.

Maureen saw a boy jump out of a police car at the ranger station, run up to a woman and little girl, and get lost in a group hug as sirens swooped and soared.

In a more subdued voice, Percy asked, "What kind of shape's the kid in? Need Jack's DNA?"

"Thirty-one?" said a new voice in the distinctive drawl of the Sheriff of Barber County. "Percy? Percy, this is Sheriff Jamie. How you doin'?"

"Hey, Jamie, how's it goin'?"

"Now, you let him go and bring yourself on in, and that gun, too, and we'll all be happy."

"Hold on, have to think about this."

Maureen saw the truck come to a stop where the meadow met the road.

"First thing, Percy, is bring him in. That makes everything better for you."

"Problem is— Well, Jamie, first problem's the gun."

"Agreed, but I'm sure we can work out how you thought you were doing a public service, and last night, man, I'm tellin' you, took *balls* to go in there in the dark, cuff those target-shooting drunks. Notice no one has a word to say about your having the gun *then*. Thought it was the damn Iraqis!"

(On Friday a car bomb in Najaf had killed more than 125.)

"OK, OK, 'cuz the gun's enough to put a two-time felon away for good—"

"'Nother case, maybe so, but this one has the extenuating circumstances. Why, we're *rejoicing* over that little boy reunited with his folks. Wouldn't you like to come in and see that for yourself?"

"Well, Jamie, and there's Jack. It took the gun to get him in my truck."

"Yeah?" asked Sheriff Jamie, sounding sad. "Well, Percy, wish you wouldn't have done that. Makes things harder."

Percy asked wearily, "So what's it look like?"

"Well, till the D.A. gets hold of it, anyway, I guess kidnapping, unless maybe just unlawful detainer—'cept you moved him, right?—and threat of deadly force, and possession of firearms by a felon.

"But here's the thing, my friend: Won't but get harder for you longer you stay out. To make things better you got to come in *now*, Percy. To make things the best they can *be*."

There was a pause, and from Percy a flat, inward statement,

spoken as if he were addressing nobody, even if he depressed the *Speak* button: "I'm not going back."

"But you *are* coming up here," commanded Mark. "Right now, Bratcher."

Percy said, "OK, 25."

And his truck, turning into the road, moved towards the booth, going the wrong direction in the exit lane, Jack at the wheel, the shotgun jammed against his neck, Lady pushing her noble head into the breeze. As they passed, Maureen and Rupert lowered themselves beneath the windowsills.

The truck stopped ten yards off. After half a minute of what looked like animated discussion, the shotgun pushed Jack's head to a steeper angle and the backup lights came on. Maureen watched it coming with dread. Rupert dropped again, but she stood her ground.

"Percy, the heck you up to *now?*" asked Mark. "Thought we agreed—"

Percy spoke into the booth.

"Come on, Maureen, get in here. Rupert can handle things here on out."

Maureen came out, went around and climbed in next to him. What else could she do? Percy groaned into the middle of the seat.

"Sorry, Maureen," Jack said.

"Not your fault," she answered past Percy.

"Percy, that's not helping," said the Sheriff, his voice rising. "Just stay where you are, let the man and woman go, we'll see what the best—"

"Seems to me I could use all the hostages I can get about now, Jamie," Percy said. "I'm looking at *life*."

"I know it," said the Sheriff.

Inside the truck no word was said until Jack ventured, "Where to?"

"Maureen's, I guess," Percy sighed. "My place is a pigsty."

Jack drove slowly past the ranger station.

On the radio Louise, the campground host, asked in a shaky, aged voice, "Sixty-seven to 25! Sixty-seven to 25! Was Site 241's reservation for tonight, too, or just last night?"

"Sixty-seven, we'll sort it out later," Mark answered. "Keep the channel clear for now."

"'Cause he has an Internet receipt, but somebody else —"

"Louise, it'll have to wait," Mark said severely.

Percy came on, laughing. "Thirty-one to 67," he said. "Don't mind Mark, Louise. He's having a *baad* day."

"Sounds like it," said the old lady. "Ten-four, Percy."

In the campground, Jack took the short, wrong way to Maureen's. A pair of police cars already there pulled back to let them jounce past unhindered.

"Watch the potholes," Maureen said as Jack eased the truck to her door.

"Hey, you need new gravel," said Percy. "Should tell Mark."

They got out on her side. Lady they left in the truck.

"This way, *faggot*," Percy said.

"Don't call me faggot," Jack replied.

"*Feisty*, he's a *feisty* faggot." They moved slowly, in a sandwich, Percy in the middle shuffling backwards, aiming the gun skyward. "Maureen, you first."

She unlocked her door and went inside. Maggie greeted her. Percy yanked the dog out, pushed Jack in, followed and slammed the door shut. Maureen's cats rolled over yawning with pleasure as they heard her return, then scrabbled to their feet and vanished.

Maureen sat down on the couch, and Jack next to her. She grabbed his hand, he clapped his other hand on top of hers, she topped it and squeezed. Neither said anything. It was chilly in there, the a/c humming, and dim. The curtains were drawn shut, but they could hear vehicles rushing up and voices issuing commands, apparently to clear the loop. Her shortwave was turned off, but Percy knew where to find it.

He fell into his old chair. Maureen saw nothing questioning about him, nothing not settled. He occupied the chair rock-like, unuprootable, legs splayed, gun angled upwards on his right, the fingers of his left hand stretching open, crabbing closed.

"Coffee, anyone?" she asked. "Iced tea?"

"Pepsi would be good," said Percy.

She got Pepsi. Taking her time, she cracked an ice tray and dropped cubes in tall styrofoam cups. She wondered at her own calm, but had a feeling that, whatever happened, it would be all right.

*Can't explain it,* she thought, *except maybe I'm so old I'm past caring. Or maybe I'm just confident in* The Code of the Bratchers: *Percy can't hurt the innocent. The innocent are safe from Percy.*

When she served, Jack at first said he didn't want any, but changed his mind, and she herself was extremely dry.

Percy said, "This is fucked up. But what could I do?"

It was an apology. To Maureen's surprise, he was imploring her. Such pity washed over her!

"Oh, *Percy,*" she said. "Just walk out the door with us!"

"Wipe the slate clean? Start over?" He smiled the broadest smile she ever saw on him, sitting with legs apart, gripping that ugly gun's chopped-off, castrated length, in control except for stray embers of hair that stood upright. "Too late. *Code of the Bratchers,* isn't that what you call it, Maureen?" His smile turned rueful. Ice chinked against teeth.

Jack was sitting still and within himself; a surprisingly serene if powerless place. He felt curious, in a detached way, about this *Code of the Bratchers.* Did it mean safety or death? He supposed the gun had to go off, but he wasn't sure.

"Percy—" he said. He didn't know what his next words were going to be.

"Hands flat on the table, *faggot,*" said Percy. "Had enough of

# THE WEDDING ON BIG BONE HILL

your lip."

"I didn't say anything."

Ker-*chunkt!* "WILL YOU SHUT THE FUCK UP?"

Jack's face went white. He took his hands off Maureen's and, leaning forward, slapped them flat on the glass-top coffee table. He had nothing to say. Percy saw it and laughed. *A gun trumps language*, Maureen thought. *Every time, bet on it.*

"Should have heard him in the truck, *yak, yak, yak*. Kid snatched, he's *insulted* I think of him."

"Well," Maureen said, "but it turns out no kid *was* snatched."

Percy sat not moving, a familiar enough sight, if not too recent a visitor, knees up like a child's, elbows decorously placed, and he had that gun sticking up from his thigh, the short barrels parallel to his face proclaiming a function radically out of place in her pretty room. The fingers of his left hand stretched open and closed.

"Takes time to set up," he said, "like any show. What'll it be? Megaphone? Tear gas? Or snipers, maybe? Cut to the bullets?"

"Come on, it's not as bad as all that," Maureen appealed. "You haven't killed anyone."

"Not yet," he said, smiling. "Not going back, though. Not for anything. Hey, *faggot*, ever tell you 'bout when they paroled me after my first stretch, 33 months, what happened?"

Jack had to work his saliva to find his voice. "No."

"Hell, Maureen, probably never told you either.

"OK, push me out the gate, *paroled*: Shitty new suit, 50 bucks in my pocket, directions to see my lady parole officer first thing. Take the 'Hound to Fort Horace, then walk it in my shiny new shoes, get fucking blisters, find the place, go on in.

"'Well, well, well,' she goes, 'so it's the tough Mr. Bratcher.' Explains the terms of my parole, everything I got to do to stay out, how if I don't follow them to the letter it's back inside for me, yada yada *yada*.

"Finally I just go, 'Finished yet, *bitch?*'

"So she puts this itsy-bitsy chrome job on me—made me laugh—and calls the cops, and they shackle me up to drive me back, only it's too late that day to admit me, there's paperwork.

"So they run themselves ragged trying to find some place *will* take me for the night, me in the backseat laughing my head off. Finally the lock-up in Osawatomie says OK, and off we go, but there's a detour, then a flat tire, it never ends.

"Spend that whole time, and the three months extra it cost me inside, thinking of the look on her face when I called her *bitch*."

Jack asked, "Was it worth it?"

"Damn *straight* it was worth it!" Percy said, staring. "No *man* would have to ask."

His hair was hiked up in ginger alarm, as if sketched from a cartoon character's. Maureen's hand ached to smooth it, though smoothing it could begin it; been known to. Percy's hand could close on hers, carry it below. Then it would be matter of fact as he took off his clothes and she took off hers, each folding what it's best to fold since no one irons any more.

It wasn't Jack's presence that inhibited her, nor was it that stranger sitting patiently by, Death in a flying visit, stealing a moment from his punishing schedule to assist and preside.

It was that the distance between them couldn't be bridged. Percy was in a place she couldn't reach, a temple devoted to his Code, to the pride of manhood reclaimed, a sanctuary impenetrably fenced by facetiousness and self-mockery, but a place of purity, too.

Percy lifted his Pepsi, and she thought he was heaving a mighty sigh, until she realized the sound came from ice sliding reluctantly along styrofoam.

"Been here before," he remarked.

"You mean with Mark, years ago?"

"*Why* didn't I just pull the fucking trigger? *Why* did I back off?"

"Because you were thinking of your wife and children, Percy."

"What a *fool* I was."

"Walk out the door with us," she repeated.

But something distracted him. Something outside claimed his attention, made him scour the whiskers of his cheek while crying, *"Oh, for Chrissake — !"* in the sepulchral tone of a man who sees his life's work gone for naught, sounding so very disappointed that Jack and Maureen turned their heads to follow. The strip of sky above the curtains showed a joyful streak of color: A kite cavorting.

After that they expected a discharge, knew second by second only the lack of it. Outdoors someone shouted something that failed to penetrate the air conditioner's hum. Percy's left hand joined his right in raising the polished stock, and the barrels began poking at his face. They smoothed his cheek, flattened his nose, pushed his upper lip aside, ducked into his mouth. His eyes looked startled, as if they couldn't believe what that gun was up to, and shot Maureen a look before her eyes rolled off his.

"Get the fuck out," he said hoarsely. "Both of you."

They were still for a moment, then moved simultaneously so clumsily the coffee table turned over. They tumbled through the door scarcely remembering to put their hands in the air, before a blast knocked one moment into the next, jangled windchimes, briefly left the water running. Jack grabbed Maureen and she grabbed back. Each at first feared the other was hit and needed assurance that it wasn't so, that they were OK and on solid earth.

Overhead a red kite and a blue were merrily looping each other.

## 30.

JACK WAS APPALLED. Also he was angry. Above all, he was *glad*—surpassingly *glad*—to be alive. But angry. And appalled.

After a debriefing by the police (also appalling), he burrowed inside the Cortez, but his fellow volunteers' kind casseroles found him there, so with Lady he embarked on a marathon walk across meadows and through woods that were beginning to batten themselves down for winter.

At sunset, he climbed to the summit of Big Bone Hill. Kansas may not be famous for its heights—the summer just past had seen controversy erupt after a scientific study found the state to be flatter than a pancake (a conclusion deeply resented by Kansans)—but he arrived at the top breathing hard. He found himself lord of an enormous landscape, cool and autumnal, clouds poised dramatically to either side of the setting sun.

Watching darkness begin to absorb everything he realized, all at once, that he was done with life on wheels, done with the *RV lifestyle*. What he had to do, the only thing he *could* do, was go back to work—drive East, settle nearer family and see what beckoned, spend the remainder of his life—*Percy's gift!*—doing the best his talents would allow, in a new access of patience. Anticlimactic, to be sure; but better at any rate than that shotgun blast he couldn't get out of his head.

"OK, girl, now I know where we're headed," he told Lady. "Let's go back."

A few days later, Maureen's friend Doug accompanied her to Travis's funeral. The mowers served as pallbearers, and almost all the volunteers attended; Dennis took the morning off from the dollar store.

But during the service it was Percy who was on her mind, and such is small-town life that, as Travis's coffin sank through the Astroturf masking the dirt that is burial's essence, Percy's body was

— THE WEDDING ON BIG BONE HILL —

being interred not 50 yards off in a ceremony attended by a radically smaller group. A burly young man with red hair might have been his son, dug up from God knows where. No sign of Donna, however. Maureen did notice Mark looking sharply over there from the group of volunteer wives he was consoling.

"*The Code of the Bratchers* saw him through," Maureen told Doug as he drove her back to the park, and it struck her that she was pronouncing Percy's epitaph. "I guess I knew it would, that's why I didn't die of fright.

"That time he faced down Mark with a deer rifle? Percy let his Code down and never escaped the consequences. An open wound that never healed. His not pulling the trigger *then*, and then, the other time, shooting at Mark with that Enfield rifle over and over and missing every time, made pride the issue it was the other day.

"He never regained his manhood" — she bracketed the word with air quotes — "as he understood the term until he did what he did. Pulling the trigger finally fulfilled him. Stuck to his Code at last. Mocked it, but followed it. Made up for his old mistake — in his mind, anyway — and gave himself the only end that could be of his choosing."

Doug patted her hand.

"So scary anyone could be that angry," she added. "Or so alone."

She sent Doug inside her trailer to salvage cat food — Maggie and the cats were already staying at his house — and a few possessions. She had no intention of setting foot inside it again herself. In fact, she meant to inquire through Mark whether a certain pair of recent arrivals might accept it as a gift despite its history. They were a hapless, very young couple living in a tent donated by a church. He was unemployed and she, pregnant, worked at Long John Silver's. Every morning he got behind the wheel of a heap wrapped in duct tape and *she* in her yellow ruffles pushed it to a start so he could drive her to work; to remonstrances, he explained she didn't drive stick.

But Maureen thought it unlikely they would accept.

Doug came out and reported that a blanket had been thrown over the mess in the living room. From his description she realized it was her grandmother's quilt that blood and brains now soiled. All right, she told herself, accept it, move on.

Next door, the Cortez roared to life.

Jack jumped out and circled it, unplugging cords and disconnecting hoses. Dennis having said that under the circumstances he wouldn't hold him to his season commitment, Jack took him up on it and returned his bank and permits, washed his motorhome and saw to the fluids and tires. For inscrutable investigatory reasons the police told him to stick around, but that morning he'd called Sheriff Jamie to say he was leaving, and the sheriff offered no demur.

Maureen hurried over, Doug following. From inside Lady saw her and pawed the door. Jack opened it, and she romped out and bobbed up to be petted.

"Not quite Eden in the end, so we're off," Jack said.

"We'll miss you both," Maureen said. "Where are you headed?"

"To visit family in the East," Jack answered. "Time to get off the road, I think. How was the funeral?"

"Sad," she answered. "Jack, have a good trip, a good winter. Keep in touch. Lady, you be a good girl."

"I promise," Jack said. "You, too. Say goodbye to Maggie for us."

They hugged. After Percy's blast they hugged for dear life. Today it was ceremonial, two self-contained people draping arms around the other, perhaps embarrassed at having shared so extreme an experience.

Jack and Doug shook hands, and Jack said, "C'mon, Lady, let's hit the road."

Ears back, Lady tore inside and jumped behind the wheel. Jack closed the door, cleared her off, she jumped on the other captain's chair and barked out the windshield.

Offering Maureen a smile, Jack honked as he steered for the horizon.

# *Junkie, Indiana*

*I know you didn't mean it
when you slit my throat,
you were just out with the fellows
trying to have some fun.*

—Mose Allison
*I Know You Didn't Mean It*

# 2018

When Fewkes sold his Ranger—he was stepping up to a used Silverado—the kid buying it insisted he remove the decal on the back window:

> *In Memory of Cordelia*
> *1997-2014*
> *My Angel's with*
> *The Other Angel's Now*

So it read, next to a lighted candle in black and white.

Fewkes complied, using a razor blade to push curls of vinyl to the truck bed under the new owner's critical eye. It only took a minute. The breeze took some of the slivers as he scraped the window clean.

*Angel?* No; Fewkes knew that was a lie. Still he couldn't avoid that stupid *Wonder what she's doing now?* familiar to every parent of a dead child.

But he knew what: Burning up in Hell, that's what—in Hell where she belonged for killing her baby and herself. She was standing in fire, flames licking along her arms and legs, flames falling off her hair and fingers, dripping off lips and nose, her mouth open in a flame-throwing scream forever and ever.

Well, she knew the rule: *Thou Shalt Not Kill.* Four little words, can't make it simpler than that. Her choice.

And her baby was—where? Surely not still in her belly in Hell? But where else? The Church abolished Limbo, so *where?*

Not that Fewkes went to church any longer, or even tried to save babies, not after Father Loomis buried Cordelia in consecrated ground next to her mother. The priest claimed it was impossible to know Cordelia's intent, and noted that Fewkes already owned the plot. But rules are rules, or nothing means anything.

The buyer grimly ran his fingers over the glass, paid Fewkes and drove the Ranger away.

Fewkes took the Silverado out to the cemetery, visiting not for Cordelia's sake, but for her mother's and the baby's. Her baby lies at rest inside its killer, but extracting it would have been *abortion.* He remembered how every time they visited her mother's grave Cordelia would smooth it, pick up any stray leaf or twig and caress the stone, determined to improve her rest. There was no stone for Cordelia; the decal had been her only monument.

Fewkes knelt for a while, imploring the heavens, then wiped his eyes and went home.

# 2014

## 1.

MONDAY BEING the babykillers' busy day, Fewkes liked to be there with his daughter, kneeling on the sidewalk outside Women's Health. A sacrifice, since Monday's a good day for scrapping, too — people drag junk out to the alleys all weekend. Fewkes worked Sundays instead, trawled behind houses the whole day, counting on God to know he meant no disrespect to His Sabbath.

They were in Louisville one warm Monday in May with eight or ten regulars. Whenever a car nudged to the curb everybody sank to their knees, Fewkes groaning.

Most of those who braved the court-mandated corridor through them were blushing young women accompanied by older ones. Fewkes drilled them as they passed, holding out his hands in appeal, his mustache overhanging the black Groucho. Since the court order, they didn't shout about the pain the unborn feel, but offered mute testimony instead, as symbolized by the electrical tape over their mouths.

Across from him kneeled Cordelia, arms bent at the elbow,

hands cupped, eyes shut, alabaster face tilted back, curly hair a vivid red. Just 16, she looked younger, but while the tape made Hitlers out of Fewkes and the others, Cordelia remained angelic, the black but a stray daub. The women tended to veer towards her, but she had a way of opening her eyes in dismay as they came closer, of steepling her hands pleadingly, that hurried them straight through the blacked-out doors.

Looking across in the wake of two women who passed as though fleeing a storm at their shoulders, Fewkes thought, *"If they can walk past my baby to kill theirs, they're just devils."* She was all he had; his wife was dead, his son in prison.

One day Father Loomis showed him an *Annunciation* and thumped Mary with his finger.

"Cordelia's spittin' image," he said. "A motherly child: That's Cord."

The love in Cord's heart encompassed both unborn babies and a certain beautiful boy. She could ignore the city's restless energies, the streams of cars and buses, the fire trucks booming past, even the screams of the slaughterhouse pigs as she gave secret voice to her heart: *"Jordan, Jordan, I love you."*

Only Louisville's municipal roadkill truck trailing its stench of shoveled-up dogs and cats could threaten her ecstatic contemplation of her beloved: *"I love you, Jordan!"*

When the two women came out again, everybody dropped to their knees once more, hands over eyes, heads bent in grief.

At 4:00 o'clock, a guard locked the doors and Fewkes scooped Cord to her feet.

"Time to go, babe."

Cord blinked as though coming out of a trance. "OK, Daddy."

They went to pump up his Ranger's tire, Fewkes smoking while the compressor chugged, then loaded up at White Castle.

Shady Acres Trailer Park overlooks the chutes and rapids of the Whitewash River Gorge in Chuterville, Indiana, two hours north of

Louisville. His truck wasn't up to the Interstate, so Fewkes took the cross-country route, striking across the Ohio River and north through open country, green fields already being groomed by gigantic combs. On the way up into the hills they passed upright brick manses standing back from the road, ranch houses carving cornfields into suburban quarter-acres and clapboard farmhouses rising amidst barns and silos, and looped several stone courthouses.

## 2.

THE NEXT MORNING Jordan stirred awake in the drizzly gloom at the barked command of Adam's phone alarm. He freed an arm from beneath his cousin, groped for and silenced the phone and, scrubbing his shorts to untangle his crotch, got up to pee.

When he returned Adam was sitting up smoking, brooding. They were staying at their skanky aunt Jasmine Stocker's trailer at Shady Acres, every night collapsing as late as they could manage on her faux-leather pullout in clouds of the diatomaceous earth she scattered against bedbugs.

Adam was stocky and not very tall, his body hairy, but at 23 (Jordan was 19) his angular head already balding, merely tufted with dark hair. He made up for it with a billy-goat beard. Three years earlier, Chuterville's young men's fashion had been to gauge the ears — pierce the lobes and spread them with colored disks — and Adam followed it. Fashion moving on, no one wore disks now, save for apologetic clear or flesh-colored ones meant to go unnoticed. Adam scorned those, as well as the surgical repairs others were resorting to; his earlobes dangled, empty loops.

"Time?" Jordan asked, pulling on yesterday's clothes. "Adam?"

"All right, all right."

Adam peed, found clothes on the floor, another cigarette for his lip, slapped on rectangular glasses. He had the use of babymama #3's old purple Honda on condition he without fail pick her up at her parents' for her shift at Walgreens; take her there and later bring her home.

As they trailed outdoors, Cordelia was watching from across the way through a window spun with spider webs that made the scene look weepy.

Though Adam was morose, Jordan snuffled with the laughter of a good-humored youth as he capered to the car in a wife-beater that showed off biceps like handgrips and soiled white jeans, something rolling at their crotch.

*Jordan,* she sighed, making the spider webs shimmer, *I love you, I love you.*

She heard Adam say, "God, do I need to get high."

Jordan snuffled a laugh and, to the rockslide sound of tires on gravel, off they went to get the babymama to Walgreens.

## 3.

FOR A QUARTER CENTURY, Adam's mother Bunny Stocker, Jordan's mother Kitty Stocker and their sister Jasmine Stocker had beguiled and terrorized the men of Chuterville in pursuits that kept life interesting, their husbands on the ball and themselves high, though they also, even as time and drugs eroded their personal charms, went to prison in regular rotation.

At the moment, Bunny was finishing a sentence at Rockville for kiting checks, but the State of Florida intended to extradite her to serve the four years for muling drugs it had sentenced her to *in absentia*. Her relatives talked gaudily of chain gangs.

Meanwhile, Kitty at long last was having some luck. She felt she deserved it.

She'd gotten out a few months earlier determined to stay out, so refused Jasmine Stocker's offer of room at Shady Acres (generous, since Kitty was responsible for Jasmine Stocker's now ex-husband's bankruptcy, hence indirectly for their divorce, having borrowed his new F-150 one day and, pulled over for speeding, crammed her crack pipe down the window groove; the resulting search, overseen by a growling K-9 unit, effectively and punitively totaled the truck).

Even Kitty's own husband, long-suffering Jordan Sr., a groundskeeper at Chuterville's country club, would have taken her back into his doublewide across town.

Instead, she rented a falling-down house—"needs TLC," the ad read—in the neighborhood across the gorge and got a job at Happy Arbors coaching the old folks through their bowel movements.

For a while Kitty seemed to be making it, but her wages, even supplemented by the pills she purloined from her charges, were not enough—not enough to keep her high—so she supplemented her income by reverting to an old pursuit: She posted her crotch shot online, a .jpeg ten years old and juicier than in life—"MILF ISO NSA FWB $$$"—and thereafter scandalized her neighbors with a daily parade of men drawn to the image of her shaven pudendum with its vermilion crack. "Hi," they'd go, jumping down from a Ram or throwing a leg over a Harley, "I'm Chuterville Sam!"

She lived alone—pointedly refused to house her son, though it was she who'd set him on his present path. Four years earlier Jordan was a sweet high-school sophomore surprising everybody with theatrical talents—just cast as George Gibbs in the school production of *Our Town*—when Kitty, already challenged with feeding her habit, had the brilliant idea of addicting him, too, to the painkillers and uppers and downers that, in intricate turnabout, kept her going (though in true maternal fashion, she refused to introduce him to heroin, her first love; Adam did that later).

Jordan played his first, and last, performance high, giggling through Grover's Corners, and then, dropping out of school, kept both himself and his mother fucked up by becoming a thief, a hustler, whatever he needed to be, whatever it took.

Fortunately, Jordan was a natural. He turned his emergent stage skills to lucrative account in stores with his fingers' golden touch and in men's vehicles and beds, besides bringing the face of an angel to the trades of burglar and strong-arm robber.

At first he easily supplied both himself and Kitty but, their wants widening—as wants will—he started hocking everything she possessed and she had to throw him out. Then a liver infection landed her in Squire Hospital, where they found her injecting heroin into her IV line; hence her return to Rockville.

Now, it was lucky and irresistible to have a project pop up in her own backyard, or just across the alleyway from it. The neighborhood, built more than a century ago for the piano factory workers—the piano factory whose ruins line the riverside—remained a working-class one, though actual workers were few and far between, but the well-kept house behind hers belonged to a very old man whom Kitty saw only when his garage door rose and he backed his not-very-new Lexus into the alley, sometimes with an ill-looking old woman sitting next to him.

Compassionate Kitty took charge on trash day of pulling her neighbor's Rosie Rollers 30 feet down his driveway to the alley and later pulling them back empty—just a neighborly gesture, amply rewarded by exchanging friendly waves with the man. Every dusting of snow that winter had her noisily dragging a shovel down his driveway. When one mild day her neighbor happened to be pottering about his yard, she showed herself in hers, tugging at her maple's dead limb, and he tottered over to thank her.

She responded vivaciously, yakking away at the poor man for half an hour. He loved it. Thereafter he made himself useful in taking her shopping (she'd driven drunk one too many times to keep her license). He took to parting from her, when safely back in his garage, with an all-hands hug and a kiss on the lips.

The sisters' tried-and-true motto was *There's no fool like an old fool*. Bunny blazed the trail, taking lonely elderly men for all she could get and generally laying them in their graves, more or less of natural causes. "He died happy, I think," she would say pensively of her latest mark.

Bunny set the gold standard when she cozied up to a millionaire widower far gone in dementia and in the last year of his life drained his assets hand over fist. She held court at his kitchen table, piled high with drugs and crowded with visitors, while the old man, outnumbered in his own home, querulously bustled about upstairs.

That season of plenty made an addict out of *her* son. Adam would drop by after school—this was soon after his father threw him out—and try a little bit of everything so copiously on offer, the Xanax, Oxycodone and Vicodin, Ecstasy, crystal meth (a favorite of the sisters' biker friends), weed, hash, cocaine in both its powder and crack-cocaine forms (crack being the sisters' guilty pleasure), and finally the one that is a way of life, heroin; once an urban drug, heroin now powders the Corn Belt.

Washed down, naturally, with whatever was going. Adam found he liked beer, bourbon, vodka, gin, tequila, rum and wine—Scotch not so much.

Bunny meanwhile had pizzas delivered five at a time, and Adam thought, *This is living.*

The episode left little but trackmarks and a souvenir photograph taken in Las Vegas, which Bunny and a boyfriend visited with the old man and his credit cards in tow. She hired prostitutes to babysit him while she and her friend lost his money at the tables (later telling everyone they won big). The photo showed him in a Scrooge McDuck T-shirt and boxer shorts printed with greenbacks (and puffed out by Depends underneath), his arms around two beaming, top-heavy young women. Under his shrewd eyes a smile cobwebbed with drool proclaimed pure joy.

As Bunny asked, Did anyone really think he'd be happier in a memory unit somewhere?

Alas, when he expired—they found him one night on his bedroom floor in the brick Tudor in Chuterville's best neighborhood, perhaps two days dead—all Bunny had to show for it was a longish term in prison.

Kitty's elderly neighbor was not so out of it, not by a long shot, and getting anything out of him was ridiculously effortful—in fact, impossible. He was a retired farmer in a region where it's farmers who have money. Kitty reminded herself of Ruth in the Old Testament story, crawling over Boaz's harvested field searching for overlooked grains of barley.

Hugs and thanks she collected tons of, but otherwise had no luck at all, aside from soda cans she found rooting through his recyclables. Once he asked her into his kitchen for a cup of coffee and introduced her to his ailing wife; Kitty wasn't again invited indoors.

One morning in May, after watching them both drive off, Kitty walked into their house. The door was unlocked, typical of Chuterville. She gave herself half an hour.

They certainly had a lot of nice things, things she longed to wheel down to the pawn shop, but she intended taking no risks. In a desk drawer in the study she came across a box of checks. She took the bottom packet of 25, and also ripped out some flimsies traced with his signature. Last, she found a statement for a brokerage account worth north of $500,000! Trembling, she got out of there.

Like her sisters, Kitty was an old hand at forging checks. She wouldn't be greedy, but go slow, make them out in small amounts to people she could trust; slow and steady would do it.

## 4.

AFTER DROPPING OFF the babymama, Adam and Jordan scored the blueberry muffin that was all their funds would extend to, though in the store Jordan also slipped a Snickers into his pocket.

They split both—Jordan happy to cede the larger halves to Adam, with whom he was in love—and returned to Shady Acres. The drizzle meanwhile strengthened to a steady pounding on the roof that filled the trailer with racket. Jasmine Stocker was snoring over the rain as they got under the pullout's blanket and fell back asleep.

Shady Acres lies off the Interstate, whose arterial hum can be heard at all hours, though no one's aware of it save when a semi crosses into opposing lanes or rolls over a minivan. Its tract was never farmed. Trees meet overhead in a dense canopy, rock shelves emerge above the riverbanks and big round stones lie scattered at random on the surface. Potholes honeycomb the lane—usually wet, often foggy—that loops through the trailer park, where 30 or 35 old mobile homes sit jammed into greenery, settled at comfortable angles and looking like moldy pastel shoeboxes.

At noontime Jasmine Stocker woke up the cousins with her gravel foghorn, coming out of her room calling, "Jordan? Hon? It's your mom."

"What's she want?"

Before answering she took a drag on her Marlboro and a chaser from the oxygen tank slung around her neck. The eldest of the sisters, she looked it. Her toothless jaw jutted like a saucer held to her chin, the shapeless sack she wore emphasizing the ruin of the rest of her. She was 44.

"Don't know," she gasped. "S'got something for you."

Jordan took the phone. "Hello?"

"Honey, I've got— How you doin'?"

"Fine, Ma, 'ra you?"

"Look, $200, do me a favor."

"*Mmm?*"

"Gentleman friend's making a gift, two checks, 500 apiece, made out to *you*."

"Yeah?"

"Cash 'em, you can keep 200."

"Mom?"

"Yes, honey?"

"Adam's sleeping. Catch you later."

It wasn't no.

When Adam finally opened a protesting eye, Jordan laid it out for him.

"Sounds OK, doesn't it?"

"I doubt the guy signed—"

"Doesn't matter, bank cashes 'em, right?" said Adam, eyes darting in shallow angles within his frames. "If somebody forged 'em, that's not *you*. All you do's sign your name in front of them. Have the right to do that, don't you?"

"I guess."

Adam crammed his anxiety about where their next high was coming from into his, "So let's go sign your name, dumbass!"

They drove to Kitty's, sat down at the wobbly kitchen table.

"Here you go, honey, Hoosier National. Should be no problem."

Holding the checks up to the light, Jordan asked for an

exemplar of the old man's signature. Kitty had done a good job.

"Why two?" he asked.

"Don't know, cleaner that way." The real answer was that she incorrectly supposed it would keep her forgeries at the misdemeanor level should things go south.

"OK," he said.

"Keep 200 for yourself, mind, and bring the rest back here."

"Two-fifty," said Jordan. "I'll bring you your money, don't worry about it."

"That's all a mother does, honey, is worry. OK, 250." Her smile showed gaps in her teeth.

Hoosier National was across town, on the strip. On the way there they passed its magisterial old downtown home carved from granite, now a thrift store, and Adam handed Jordan reds and blues from his sacred wallet stash. Jordan required something to help stifle his innate sweetness; pills helped purpose to form inside him.

They also passed a well-known local martyr shouldering his 12-foot wooden cross down the sidewalk, rolling it on the little rubber wheels Jesus never thought of.

Adam swung into the bank's parking lot and lit a cigarette while Jordan got out wearing a young man's armor—his hoodie—and went inside glassy-eyed and blank-faced, moving like an automaton.

It was half an hour before closing time. At a table he took out the checks and picked up a pen. The first one he tried was dry, but the second one worked, he endorsed both checks and, suppressing any curiosity about his surroundings, careful especially not to stare into a ceiling camera, took them to the counter.

He produced his I.D., it was inspected and notes taken, consultations made, a shrug delivered, and $1,000 counted across. In addition, a smile—a bank's reflexive tribute to cash—was thrown in for free.

Jordan's step had a bounce as he returned to the Honda.

Jordan knew Adam well enough to insist on going back to his mom's with her share before visiting Dopeman, but they had a nice night even so. An outstanding night, actually, for they splurged on speedballs—heroin and cocaine combined.

A memorable night, save that next morning they couldn't remember much of it, and found it particularly painful to get up at the alarm's summons to take the babymama to work, and lacked money even for a muffin.

## 5.

CHUTERVILLE OFFICIALLY opened its new hospital on Memorial Day. Unofficially, it had begun operating weeks earlier as patients and departments were transferred from the old one.

The new Squire Hospital was placed farther outside town, a hilltop sprawl of steel and glass. The portrait of the millionaire who endowed it in robber-baron days was carried with ceremony to the new palace's lobby, where his sclerotic gaze could bless the modern-day sick. A tent was raised in the parking lot, a 5K walk/run held, refreshments served, tours offered and a ribbon cut by the town's leading committeewomen.

Fewkes could hear the high-school band—the Marching Devils—over loudspeakers as he pushed his truck through a woods lane and across a lawn already in need of mowing to reach the abandoned hospital from behind. It was a rambling jumble of architectural styles, the original 1900 stone block dwarfed by 1920s brick wings and the glassy pavilions added in 1960.

— *JUNKIE, INDIANA* —

It was deserted, as he'd hoped. Or almost so: A car stood near the front doors, presumably a security guard's. As Fewkes walked cautiously around the structure, pry bar in hand, trying doors, he could see someone sitting near the entrance, raised legs silhouetted against greenery on the other side.

Finally forcing a door at the loading dock, Fewkes was inside.

Moving at first with caution, then more boldly, he tramped the corridors unable to believe his luck: The hospital was empty but intact. It was Ali Baba's cave. Hallways led past ward after empty ward, five stories of them—*intact*. Turn the lights back on and you could admit patients.

"Holy shit," he repeated with glee, strutting like a king through a captured castle or a Dark Ages peasant through the local Roman temple after the priests decamped. The mother lode; it would take *years* to salvage everything of value. His own personal shopping mall, and he didn't know where to begin in sacking it.

The timing was right, for the enormous Continental Fixtures plant where his grandfather and father worked and whose ruins had long supplemented his income—a sprawling complex built by that selfsame Squire that for a century produced more bathtubs, lavatories, faucets and toilets than any place on earth—was at long last, like even the richest mine in time, about played out.

Shift change at the factory was the memorable phenomenon of Fewkes's youth: Automotive mayhem, cars pouring out of the lots for minutes on end, the Christmas rotation of traffic lights over the exit lanes meaningless.

But manufacturing had moved to China 25 years earlier—the brand name was still global, but now *Made in China* was impressed in stainless steel or porcelain beneath an updated, stylized C and F. Fewkes's father, then not 50, had lost his job. His foreman tried to explain capital's requirements to him—how capital must be free to go where it finds the highest return, a *diktat* of Nature's as ineluctable as water's flowing downhill; how, in the bigger picture, closing down in the U.S.A. to open up in China was a *good* thing.

Fewkes's old man didn't get it; but judging from the company's buoyant stock price and robust dividends, the move to China was prescient.

All Fewkes knew was that where once there were jobs for everybody in Chuterville, now there were none. His dad had owned his own home, two cars, a hunting cabin and bruited the idea of college for Fewkes (who, in the event, quit high school to race dirt bikes). Everything but the house went away with the job; it took another ten years for it to go into foreclosure.

But Fewkes had mined that old factory ever since. Its square mile contained gigantic lofts stretching along railway sidings, a foundry, a brass-finishing plant, its own dynamo, administration buildings and towering warehouses bedecked with fierce stone eagles. For years after it closed, a good day's work was as easy as driving past the bullet-sprayed FOR SALE billboard, albeit with ladders ever taller, and pulling conduit off the wall to get at the copper wiring within, or ripping out pipes, or prying up tracks, or smashing the remaining machinery to portable chunks and trucking it all to the scrapyard.

Even with the work of breaking things up or burning off insulation, plus the necessity of keeping an eye peeled for cops, it was easy money. There was always something to be hauled off to the scales where, not looking too close, they paid cash. The scrap value of America's Industrial Age kept Fewkes going, him and his kids; the factory was the meal ticket for generations.

Now fire had collapsed several structures and the basements of others were flooded. But little of value remained, anyway, except for sawed-off ends of copper pipes tauntingly embedded in concrete. Fewkes knew guys who lately were prying bricks out of walls or pulling down rafters and selling them as barn timber. The easy money was long gone.

In the hospital, he located the room in Obstetrics where his wife died delivering their daughter. Fewkes refused to have a beef with God but, since he had to start somewhere, started there—opening walls and yanking wires, wresting fixtures off ceilings, tugging at pipes. In fact, he demolished it.

A project like this made him miss his son acutely, but Junior had another 19 years to go in prison. A hulking youngster, rather sweet, though definitely not the brightest, he'd been expelled from Chuterville High for being thought a threat by those who, having failed to teach him to read or write, imagined resentment on his part. That his beefy arm was tattooed with the Confederate battle flag, and thus an incitement to his black classmates, didn't help. Junior was out and adrift by the age of 16.

The one thing school had given him was a girlfriend, fond of him less for his sake than because his bulk scared people. A few years later, when her latest secret flame lost interest, she talked Junior into a home invasion, and gave him the gun.

It was a big mess. After his arrest, feeling he'd at least enacted some gallantry, he accepted a plea agreement that imprisoned him for 15 years. Fewkes would have despaired, save that not long after his transfer to Michigan City from Chuterville's showcase jail Junior told his father on the phone, "Dad, I got *myself* into this predicament."

So Fewkes had hope for him still; but, oh, how he could have used his help in pulling apart the old hospital!

He might bring Cordelia next time. She could do some good.

Though for Fewkes scrapping was a never-ending treasure hunt, Cord hated the dirt, the smells, the rusty edges, dreaded coming across maggots or dead animals. Even an armload of copper gave her no joy.

But the bewilderments of high school—Fewkes insisted she wasn't *slow* so much as *late*—had caused her to drop out during the winter just past, and he thought it time she did more than babysit at a few bucks a throw or lie around the trailer begging him to get her a cat. Cats suck the breath out of babies, he informed her, he wouldn't have one in the house. So she pouted.

Fewkes filled the Ranger's bed with steel and copper, and secured a tarp over it with bungee cords; both the scrapyard and Chuterville Recycling were closed until Tuesday, and he had no wish to advertise his find and have others jump his claim.

## 6.

THE POLICE CAME to arrest Kitty early on a trash day. One cruiser blocked the alley, another parked at her front door.

She knew the officers who knocked. After glancing at the warrant, she asked to use the bathroom, and hastily combed her hair, swallowed some pills and stuffed others in a baggie up her vagina, cavity searches not being the Chuterville jail's strong point. It was a relief to find that somehow her billfold held the $30 she'd need to buy whites to go under the orange jail jumpsuit. The jumpsuit was free.

As they drove her off, she saw with complacency her elderly neighbor's Rosie Rollers standing in the alley beside hers. The old coot would have to pull them up the drive all by his lonesome.

At the jail they booked her and added a mugshot to her gallery of them. In this one, face drawn, she just looked sad, but at least her stringy hair was combed.

For the rest of the day she sat in an interrogation room, putting together what happened from what was asked of her: The old man noticed the out-of-sequence checks in his bank statement and, with more acuteness than you have any right to expect from a

90-year-old, guessed the payee to be related to his neighbor and that he'd been had. He called the police and told them to throw the book at 'em, and so Kitty found herself in a mirror-walled room being grilled by a detective.

Chuterville spent millions on its new jail, placed prominently next to the landmark courthouse. From the outside it's a well-proportioned structure of brick with white-stone facings and large expanses of glass. Indoors, one finds the windows to be fake. There's little natural light amidst overmuch steel.

There was no point in denying anything, so Kitty admitted everything, including her son's part. In fact, she played up Jordan's role: She said his addiction to heroin and pills and consequent need for cash gave him the idea of conning her neighbor. It was *Jordan's* idea; *he* made her steal the checks and knew they were forged when he took them to the bank.

Accepting a cigarette from the detective, Kitty expressed the hope that making statements about her son would help her, and he said maybe so, but being on parole, she'd now have to serve out her original sentence and probably more. Anyway, that was up to the judge.

Kitty announced she wouldn't fight anything because, after all, jail's a good place to get clean. Her piety bored them as much as it did her. They placed her in a cell with a woman who spoke only Spanish, and that night she huddled on her bunk's thin pad beneath a thin blanket, trying without much success to sleep, although because of her timely provision of pills she didn't immediately become dopesick.

## 7.

THE POLICE WENT for her son before noon the next day.

Cruisers rolled into Shady Acres and surrounded Jasmine Stocker's trailer (she was off selling her June food stamps). As the cops bore in on Jordan, his cousin padded off to find a cigarette. Jordan pulled on jeans and a shirt, and by the time they finished reading him his rights was cool and distant, fastening his belt with a bounce on the balls of his feet. They cuffed him and put him in a car, a cop paternally pushing his head beneath the headliner.

Jordan mustered his hardest look for his mugshot, but looked merely adorable, if upset and apprehensive. Unlike his mother, he lacked money for his whites so, after his picture and prints were taken, pulled on a jumpsuit over bare skin and was put into an interrogation room.

The charges, he heard, were two Class "C" felony counts of forgery.

"*Forgery?*" he protested. "You're saying *me* signing *my* name is *forgery?*"

They asked who put him up to it. This he refused to say. Of course, he knew his mother was languishing elsewhere in the jail, so was not entirely surprised when a detective quoted Kitty on its being his idea in the first place. He bled through stab wounds of betrayal, but let *her* talk, his standards were higher. He denied everything.

Finally a TV and VCR were rolled into the room and the bank's surveillance tape played. Again and again Jordan watched a jerky stop-time loop that showed a hooded figure approaching a counter and exchanging checks for cash. Shaking his head, he declared that whoever it was, it certainly wasn't *him*, and could he please have a lawyer?

Some time later a plump, distracted man in a jacket that needed cleaning and trousers that didn't match the jacket came in, sat down and took a case file and paper sack out of his briefcase.

"Jordan? Mitch Hurst, public defender." He brought out a peanut-butter and jelly sandwich, and—murmuring, "You don't mind?"—chewed while he riffled through papers, finally asking, "This your first arrest?"

"Yes, sir."

"Now, I've reviewed the charge sheet and your interview, and seen the bank video, too." He licked his fingers, looking at Jordan almost with admiration. "Got you cold, my friend—'C' felony, two counts. Have to plead you. Go to trial, you'll get four-to-six *years*. First offense, should be able to plead to four, six *months*, or even no time at all, assuming you're willing to talk about your mother. Believe me, she's singing like a bird about *you*."

Jordan declared he'd never speak against his mom, and repeated his existential protest that even if he *had* signed the checks, which he hadn't, surely signing his own name couldn't be *forgery*.

They put him in a cell already occupied by a shaven-headed man of 30 bursting his jumpsuit with limbs tattooed blue and green, and he quailed in dismay until the guy turned out to know Adam.

If he still quailed, it was with incipient dopesickness.

### 8.

ADAM WAS BUMMED when the police dragged Jordan away. He called Jordan's father to tell him about it. Jordan Sr. heaved a sigh and said he'd see about bail, but not that day—a night in jail never hurts. (In the end, he decided bail would just be enabling.)

When he came out of the trailer, Adam found Cordelia sitting on the steps.

"Move it, Cord."

"I saw the police," she said. "What happened, Adam?"

"Ask the pigs."

"Why'd they take Jordan away?" she quavered.

"Something about his mom."

"*Please* tell me." Head at crotch level, she burst into tears, hands flying to her face.

Adam liked the scent of vulnerability.

"*Aww,* Cordelia, you like him, don't you?" he said, pulling her to her feet and hugging her. Firm breasts brushed his middle.

Adam was a success with women. He found that though they think they want something pretty, all they need is something that works, and that there's something persuasive, even unanswerable, about an erection.

Patting Cord's back and bussing her hair, he brought his face around, meaning to force his tongue into her mouth and carry her hand to his crotch.

But to his astonishment she melted out of his arms.

"Come on in," he said. "Find you a Kleenex, tell you all about it."

"I don't think so," she said.

"Your dad home?" Rhetorical; he could see the truck.

"Yes."

"Take a walk in the woods?"

"I have to go home," she said, and scooted across the lane.

He watched her ass working her jeans, then got in the Honda and drove out into the countryside. He could think better behind the wheel.

WITHIN MINUTES, beginning to feel strung out, Adam was skimming past goldenrod and purple chicory, past cornfields starting the seasonal shift in perspective that by August buries you by the height of the stalks.

*How the fuck was he going to get high?*

He paralleled the bike path towards Sidestep, Ohio. His second little job in the industry was to pedal bricks of hash into town along that rail trail.

That was shortly after he'd taken his first job, when Bunny's fleeting cornucopia of drugs awakened appetites that demanded feeding and he'd become a runner, one of several kids recruited to take up positions on a sidewalk after school and study a cell phone. Whenever a text arrived, he would jolt to attention and shake the hand of the next person to walk past, in one smooth motion delivering the goods and collecting the cash, and return to studying his phone.

That first job, however, lasted only days before a fellow recruit, questioned by police, began bawling and snitched out the boss.

Adam had started out destined for something better. Where his aunts married dim men with low-paying jobs they barely managed to hang on to, his mother married a man with a future, at 20 already on an upward climb in the auction business.

Bunny proved no help to her husband's career—quite the opposite; every step of his success incited her. Bad checks drew a two-year sentence, followed by three years for selling marijuana and barbiturates. When Adam was 10, Bunny's drugs, boyfriends, thefts from her husband and others, not to mention her prison terms, finally caused his father to divorce her.

He intended to raise his son himself. Consequently, Adam (Jordan, too) grew up in the enchanted atmosphere of a small-town auction house. Dirty, funky, crammed to the rafters with a revolving inventory of junk and treasures, Off-Ramp Auctions occupied an old livery stable where sparrows flitted overhead. Three nights a week a hundred cars parked outside and indoors a fairground atmosphere prevailed.

Adorable in checked sportshirt and clip-on bowtie, Adam would run up and down the aisles with whatever antique milk can or miniature windmill was on the block, or dart around pointing out bidders as his dad spoke in tongues from the rostrum. Occasionally he would check on Jordan, stuffed in a playpen or crib being hammered off later (once one sold while Jordan napped in it, and the buyer protested that she thought the little angel came with it). Sellers operated in perpetual dismay, at the end of an evening quietly collecting their take and vanishing, while buyers, giddily triumphant, importantly maneuvered their prizes away.

Both boys loved it—the phonograph records of shellac and vinyl, the hi-fi sets, early computers, musty books, artifacts unimaginably older: crank-wound Victrolas with wax cylinders; stereoscopic viewers springing photographs into three dimensions; player pianos worked by ragtime-happy ghosts.

When Jordan was older, Adam would sit him down at some desk not due to go till late and he'd beguile himself for hours with some family's picture albums—picnics, graduations, wakes and Christmases from a century past.

A local economy in long-term decline helped Adam's dad prosper. There were always those selling up to move to Florida or those who, so as to put food on the table, at last were letting go of grandma's tea set or grandpa's portrait. By dint of exploiting the farm and house foreclosures, car and harvester repossessions, every financial calamity that could befall his fellow Hoosiers, and expanding in timely fashion to the Web, Adam's dad made money—big money. His famous antique-tractor sales always drew a covey of private jets to Squire Field. Cash was king, too, ready in its clever way to elude the tax man.

When Adam was in tenth grade his father broached the idea of a future partnership. Adam expressed excitement and began stealing from him. As a future partner he didn't think of it as theft when he went home with his pockets (Jordan's, too) filled with military medals, glass insulators, model cars.

After an antic sale one Friday, Adam was idly revolving on an antique swivel chair, waiting for his father to emerge from the inner office and take them home, when he regarded the ancient safe. Its doors were open, revealing a stack of shallow trays locked in place, each with a front cutaway allowing a peek at the contents.

He saw money in one drawer, and suggested that Jordan try to get it. Kneeling, Jordan worked in his thin blue-veined wrist and brought out four $10 bills flapping between index and middle fingers.

Adam cackled aloud. Calling, "OK out here, buddy?" his father came out and caught Jordan with his hand too literally in the till.

He lost it. Enraged, he banned both boys and threw his son out of the house. Moving back in with his mother, Adam soon graduated to serious addictions. Uninterested in high school's regimen of humiliation, he dropped out and became a runner.

When that job vanished prematurely, he began cycling hash into town, then, getting his driver's license, drove it in along I-70 or, whenever that grew hot, U.S. 40, the original National Road where ancient taverns picturesquely crowd the pavement's edge. Soon he earned a retail bench of his own on the gorge trail below the high school for the lucrative lunchtime trade, pitbull napping at his feet.

Around that time Adam made a career decision meant to preserve his personal liberty: Rather than try to become a drug kingpin, deal on a scale that would earn him a Lincoln Navigator like his boss's—with a sound system whose bass *"Motherfucker!"* could shake whole neighborhoods to dust—he would furnish friends and friends only, with the modest objective of netting enough to supply himself and Jordan while staying off law enforcement's radar. Not for him the posse or flashy ride, or the inevitable downfall, either; he just wanted to stay toasty.

It worked for quite some time. Every day without fuss Adam got high and Jordan got high. He was envied, and knew it.

"I've got an edge up, is what it is," he liked to say, sitting back and popping his dark eyes open beneath his glasses. "Like dope? Get it for free. Girls? More than I can do. Sleep in? *Do* it. See it? *Take* it. Want it? *Mine*. Got an edge up. Did I already say that?"

Part of that edge lay in his cousin's adoration. Jordan's earliest memories, from when he was 3 or 4 and his cousin 7 or 8, were of Adam's taking care of him—being fed or made to nap, or tagging along as he stole yard tools from a neighbor's garage or unhooked a tail-wagging dog from its chain and chased it onto the highway.

From a pretty boy Jordan became a handsome young man with good features, good teeth (unusual in their family) and—his pride—a large dangle. However, he retained a boy's sweetness, too, a lurking warmth that yet threatened to make him a loser.

No such fate was in store for Adam: The lessons of the drug trade reinforced those of the auction house to make him cynical.

But Adam observed that, of everyone, it's most often the cynic who succeeds. The auction trade, endlessly recycling stuff thrown off by fortune's treadmill? Cynical from start to finish.

The very word *cynic*, he thought, has a twist to it that corkscrews through bullshit, prevents the cynic alone from getting bogged down. The cynic *knows* life's shit! Everything Adam did, he did in service to a tried and tested philosophy. No one behaved more sincerely.

For instance, at 23 he had four children by three women, which meant he didn't dare get a job, for anything he earned would be garnished for child support. Though Adam proclaimed that he loved his kids, he saw them as little as possible and was insulted by the notion that because he'd slept with their mothers—his enthusiastic partners—he should be held financially responsible. "That's *fucked*," he said.

As it was, he had to spend an inordinate amount of time paying attention to his babymamas just to keep them from filing on him.

"Women are shit," he liked to say.

"But they can't help it!" Jordan would chime in. Their little routine made everyone laugh.

Adam remained on sufficiently good terms with babymamas #1 and #3, but had lost touch with Babymama #2. She turned out—*after* the fact—to resent how in her ninth month Adam raised the money that kept them high until she dropped the kid: He posted an online ad offering the services of a very pregnant girl, and that night all he had to do was manage the queue on the staircase, admit a new john every ten minutes, say goodbye to the old one, and stuff cash in his pockets.

She gave his baby up for adoption and moved away; Adam heard she was now a prostitute in Indy.

Lately, though, Adam's edge seemed to be going blunt.

He knew the risk run by the dealer who uses—*Never get high on your own supply*, goes the adage—but assured himself that awareness is half the battle, that since he'd managed for years now, he'd continue to.

But his and Jordan's love for the American Pharmacopeia—far dearer than the American Songbook—was shattering his business model. They had to have heroin, of course, because who uses it must; but it was the painkillers, the downers, the uppers, the ganja, the exotic new mixed with the standby old that they reveled in.

But using expanded their needs. The cousins could swallow, inhale, inject and otherwise ingest quantities that even a year earlier would have put them in the ground. For instance, where Squire Hospital might mercifully ease a terminal cancer patient's pain with five milligrams of morphine, Adam's tolerance for opioids meant it took 50 mg. to make itself felt. Consequently, the profits of his enterprise no longer defrayed the expenses, and that day's dilemma of how to get high was becoming all too familiar.

Necessarily, he'd begun shorting his customers/friends and as a consequence losing them. In addition, overdoses, imprisonment, flight—even, in one or two cases, a determination (however doomed) to escape addiction—thinned their ranks.

Hence Adam, like Kitty before him, was dependent on Jordan's talents as a thief for getting what he needed.

Jordan, carrying his angel face into Kmart, could tear the tag off a package of Angry Birds bedsheets, take it to the return desk and collect its price, no questions asked. Or he could stroll into Walmart and try on pants and more pants until he stalked out of the store with Tin Man's stiff gait, four new pairs under his own.

When even Jordan's thievery faltered, they relied on such absurd but necessary shifts as poking a finger in the Domino's deliveryman's back and lifting his cash (and the double-cheese in his hands), or taking in pets offered "free to a good home" on Craigslist and selling them; easier in the case of dogs than cats, though the unsalable, let loose in the countryside, were free to find hospitable barns.

THUS, AS HE DROVE PAST the cornfields and alpaca farms, puppy mills and soybean fields, swerving to avoid the bodies of deer smeared over the lanes or raccoons leaking stuffing like teddy bears, Adam wondered: *How the fuck am I going to get high?*

Rubber from burnouts and donuts imprinted every crossing. A Firebird began tailgating him, driven by a boy whose head as he blasted past looked like the bust of an infant Roman emperor. Adam accelerated, but soon gave up the chase. The Honda sounded good, but wasn't as fast.

With surprise he found himself on County Line Road. That was where, rid of wife and son and soon remarried, his father built his palace. Adam had never been inside; his father wouldn't allow him on the premises.

The house rose well off the road, a McMansion of stone and brick beneath a high, sheltering roof. It commanded a gentle slope, trees crowding around, in front a pond. An eight-foot fence of wrought iron stretched around it at incredible length. Adam always thought a picket fence would look better.

For he came out rather frequently, though never before so unconsciously. Pulling up at the next farm track, he sat studying his father's mansion, stewing with jealousy and pride. It dominated the landscape like a medieval castle. As he watched, a man atop a mower emerged from behind the house and began cutting grass along the pond's verge as though there were nothing on earth he would rather be doing. It was his father.

Feelings churning, Adam watched him stripe the turf, then sped back to town.

## 9.

AFTER TAKING his babymama home from Walgreens, Adam did what he had to do and drove on to Dopeman's.

When Dopeman got out of prison, where he atoned for knocking down his grandmother and burglarizing her neighbors, his first act was to get his face tattooed. Ever after as he rose to prominence in Chuterville's drug trade scatterbombing his *"Fucks!"* he resembled an undersized Maori warrior.

He had no more mercy for others than for himself. He never extended credit—never—but loved to be asked for it; would gravely hear out the request and sympathetically probe the situation, invariably serious, before shaking his head with a grin and in a put-on Pakistani accent saying, "Dopeman say, *Fuck!* No credit."

So today. Dopeman heard out his old friend Adam, grinned and went, "Dopeman say, *Fuck!* No credit."

Adam drove off with a contemptuous *splat!* of exhaust. He went through the roster of Chuterville dealers. No one could know them all, for like dandelions new ones were always sprouting up and old ones blowing away — or landing in jail, the local police being rather competent at noticing the extra traffic at drug dealers' houses and sending in undercover buyers for the buy-and-bust. But Adam knew as many as anyone.

East Side Orrie came to mind. Adam hated East Side Orrie for having once witnessed him inject another dealer's speedball that turned out to be baking soda and laughing, "Dude, thought you were the *smart* cousin?" Still, he called him up and made a deal, arranging to meet in front of his house in downtown's neighborhood of dilapidated mansions.

Adam drove up, Orrie came out shirtless, a twist of stainless steel through each nipple, and with an infuriating *know-about-you* smile leaned into the Honda, thrusting out his hand. Protocol, of course, called for Adam to meet that hand with his own, money folded in its palm, their handshake invisibly transferring the goods.

Orrie was saying, "Hear the pigs got your *boyfriend* —" when his eyes registered the unthinkable sensation of his heroin slipping into Adam's empty grasp even as the Honda jumped ahead, leaving him stunned and shouting, *"Fuck!"*

If Jordan were with him, Adam thought as he returned to Jasmine Stocker's, he wouldn't have to rip off East Side Orrie, an act that might have consequences. But Jordan was in jail.

He hefted the bag. Its weight made him tingle. He reminded himself that he should cut it, divide it, sell it to buy more, keep for himself only enough to forestall getting sick. But the powder shifting in his fingers insisted that tomorrow could look after itself, that *Jordan in jail!* called for indulgence.

Whereas Jordan cultivated a single trackmark, albeit an inflamed and swollen one painful to use, Adam dotted his limbs liberally, though he refused to inject tongue or penis. Tying up, he found a likely patch between toes.

O, the glamour of the needle! Injecting, he met the heavy press and blankness of stupefaction, a seizure not of joy—alas, never of *joy*—but of something all-pervading that put life's shit at a distance and quelled that pain waiting to jab him like a toothache's unconsidered breath. Secure in its hold, he curled up on the couch.

That evening, Jasmine Stocker breathing stertorously—having wheedled an aunt's share of stupefaction—and *Sons of Anarchy* disregarded on the TV, a motorcycle roared into Shady Acres.

At first she took it to be part of the TV soundtrack, then as it thundered at her door worked to her feet and peered outdoors.

"What's East Side Orrie want?" she asked. "Adam?"

The bike revved again and again. Adam was indifferent. Jasmine Stocker let fall the curtain and resumed her chair. After a sustained and threatening crescendo, the bike roared off.

When he thought about it later, Adam giggled.

## 10.

AFTER SIX DAYS of sweating, trembling, throwing up and diarrhea that had his cellmate cursing him out (but that kept him at bay), Jordan so wanted out of jail that he agreed to a version of events that blamed his mother for stealing the checks.

He signed a plea deal—Hurst pleased with his handiwork—and confirmed it to a judge at a hearing to which they walked him shackled hand and foot, his cock, given his lack of underwear, snagging the jumpsuit's crotch, and found himself a felon on probation for two years. (Kitty was remanded to Rockville to complete her original term, plus two years more.)

They bustled Jordan outdoors the same dark afternoon. The clothes he put on—what he was wearing at his arrival, ranker for being balled up since—smelled, but a drizzle damped down the stench as he hiked out to Shady Acres. Dopesick for days, he was feeling merely shaky by the time he came up the marshy lane.

Seeing him, Cordelia rushed outdoors.

"Jordan, you're out, you're out!" she cried. "They let you go!"

"Hey, Cord, how's it going?" He let her hug him and, nesting his chin on her fiery hair, found himself closing his eyes and sighing. He knew all about her crush. "Hey, let me breathe a little!"

"Oh, *Jordan!*"

Detaching himself via tactful pats on her shoulder, he went into Jasmine Stocker's trailer. On the couch Adam was hunched over in skivvies, smoking.

"Hey man," said Jordan.

"Hey man, you're out?"

"I'm out."

"Man, I'm not holding and I owe East Side Orrie. Think he's coming for it."

"Oh man, don't worry."

Jasmine Stocker came in hoisting a bottle of Colt 45.

"Calls for celebration!" she said. "Thought you were gone for good, baby doll!"

"Nah," Jordan said happily. "Probation."

They passed the malt liquor while he cheerfully told jailhouse tales—who of their acquaintance sported a surprisingly big dick in the showers, who managed to get high every day, who was being pussied out.

One friend had arrived two days previous, captured after an already legendary eight weeks on the lam—not that he went anywhere, just ran into the woods behind his buddy's whenever cops came nosing around. Finally someone saw him and tackled him, but already the word was out that men with guns had visited the tackler and, wisely, he was planning a move out of town.

Jordan was glad to be out, but also glad to have been in; he felt more of a man.

When Jasmine Stocker used the bathroom he slipped in beside Adam.

"Cut it out," Adam said. "Told you, I'm dry. Got jack shit."

Jordan didn't want to mess him up by mentioning that he was himself painfully clean and with any encouragement willing to try to stay that way. One of Adam's funniest party turns was his fast-forward imitation of Frank Sinatra going cold turkey in *The Man with the Golden Arm*; he wouldn't be sympathetic.

This first hour of wakefulness after the post-getting-the-babymama-to-work nap was Adam's agenda-setting time, when Jordan regarded his pronouncements with the awe due an oracle's.

From the moment he woke up, Adam concentrated on how to get fucked up, and by nightfall had always done it, though occasionally delaying too late to prevent on Jordan's part an episode of nausea or the runs. From morning on, Jordan's bodily functions threatened to go wrong; his digestion, especially, was chancy, reflux a daily visitor. Always, except when high, he was on the verge of being ill.

Adam breathed out the last of the smoke. "Let's go to Kitty's."

"Mom's?"

"Sell the air conditioners."

With Kitty away, and no new tenant, it was easy. They broke in, wrested both units out of the windows, trundled them to the scrapyard, and that night had $50 to enjoy. Ample; years ago, a junkie might have had a $100-a-day habit, but what with the war on drugs, they're cheaper now.

Next day the boys were back to put the fridge and range up for sale on Craigslist. Didn't take long, and after helping their buyers load up their bargains, it was off to Dopeman's.

But salvaging what remained in Kitty's house after that was laborious. A few days later they were pulling the fuse box off the wall when there was a *pop!* and an electrical sizzle. Adam laughed to see smoke escaping from, of all places, wall sockets and light switches. It was like a cartoon.

"Got to blow, bro!" he yelled.

And that day's only joy was watching the house burn down. The cousins went to bed sustained by yesterday's residue and emergency recourse to the pills in Adam's wallet.

## 11.

AN ACCURATE ACCOUNTING of Chuterville's economy today—including the casket factories and the dog-food plant—would likely reveal its biggest component to be *drugs*. To all intents and purposes Chuterville, Indiana, is a narcopolis.

But aside from whatever of true comfort drugs can offer, no benefit accrues to the town from the fact. No drug money stays in Chuterville, and in order to raise it in the first place, neighbor preys upon neighbor. The old model whereby the bathtub-makers spent their wages on goods made by other workers, and everybody had work and money—a model that powered the national economy—has collapsed. A large proportion of Chuterville's population wakes up with neither money nor work, but desperate to get high and prepared to do whatever it takes.

J.P. Morgan never meant it this way. If all anyone wants now is something to get them through the day, something to take the edge off, that's not his fault. It was Morgan who in 1894 put together the consortium that set Chuterville going on its long reign of prosperity. Morgan's talent for supercharging the American will to wealth, matching money to potential, arose in the first place from his confidence in American confidence. Alas, that national trait appears to be rusting away with its factories.

It started thus: A small but ambitious maker of patent plumbing devices, Jeremiah Squire, went to New York and approached Morgan with a proposition that would take advantage of Chuterville's location on the Whitewash River, its nexus of rail lines, its sand and clay quarries and gas wells.

Morgan took the scheme in hand. He made capital available and dispatched a partner to Chuterville to help forge Squire Plumbing and several local enameled-ironware manufacturers into Continental Fixtures, Incorporated.

Installed as its President, Squire built a vitreous-china sanitary-ware factory on the largest scale. The smokestacks and leaning water tower still display in sun-faded script the original, flamboyantly intertwined *CF* logo (Fewkes aches to get his hands on that water tower!).

Morgan even condescended to make an appearance at the groundbreaking. After plunging a gilded shovel into dirt and tapping a cornerstone with a golden trowel, he received the Chuterville *Chronicle*'s reporter in the parlor of his private railway car.

A copy of the resulting issue hangs behind glass in Squire Library: Fancy devices in colored inks frame photographs of the groundbreaking and a sepia engraving of Morgan, a far-seeing glint to his eye, his nose's famous inflammation lost in shadow. (Unfortunately, the only candid shot of him taken in Chuterville was too blurry to publish, the surprised plutocrat all proboscis as he brought down his walking stick.)

Morgan spoke to the reporter about bringing the blessings of industry to Chuterville. To local initiative, he growled, he was adding New York money and expertise, and the result would be modern plumbing fixtures for a nation fond of its comforts and sanitation. No longer must Americans import them from England or Germany; henceforth, Indiana U.S.A. would manufacture the best in the world.

And so it proved. A successful stock offering and 75 years of expansion followed. Hundred-car trains thundered in daily with raw materials, daily departed carrying gleaming product across the country and the globe. Chuterville's pall of smoke, the index to CF's prosperity, became famous, clear days an unlamented rarity in the decades when everybody in town had a job, there was a yearly influx of workers, and construction of houses, stores, schools and churches never stopped.

Largely it was proud people from the Appalachians who swelled the town's workforce. Although maps may place that range many miles to the south, Chuterville represents one of its northern reaches; Fewkes's grandparents arrived from West Virginia during World War II, when CF churned out military goods by the carload.

Continental Fixtures made its investors and executives rich. Besides endowing the hospital, library, symphony orchestra and art museum, they raised the finest courthouse in Indiana, where courthouse-building was a competitive sport—a granite chateau seemingly transported from the Loire Valley. (Meanwhile CF's corporate headquarters rose in New York, a Union Square skyscraper of gleaming white terracotta, still compared by some—not very cleverly—to a urinal.)

So things went until around 1970, when they started to go awry and CF began to lose market share. The expensive excursion of the Viet Nam war was financed through deficits, and partly as a result certain elements of the country began to delaminate; layers heretofore glued together as in plywood adhered no longer, began to peel apart, there wafting between the layers a breeze called *inflation*. Prices rising uncontrollably, demand for CF products fell.

— *JUNKIE, INDIANA* —

There ensued a generation of corporate cost-cutting and layoffs, until, in order to save the company, production moved to a new facility in Hainan Province and the Chuterville factory closed — overnight putting its last 6,000 employees out of work. CF's CEO at the time, working from leafy glades near Danbury, Connecticut, compared himself favorably to J.P. Morgan.

Chuterville has suffered ever since. The population sifts downward every year, leaving in place those who lack the gumption or means to move where the economy's more dynamic, and it seems that all the remnant can do is to pick at the town's skeleton. More houses burn than are built.

Descendants of Jeremiah Squire occasionally visit his tomb in Chuterville, and they decry what's become of the town. They no longer live there, of course, but neither do they occupy the palaces the first monied generation raised in Greenwich and Southampton. Today the Squires are scattered from Desert Island, Maine, to La Jolla, California, prospering in the professions or in business, not to mention with their inherited stock in Continental Fixtures. If their names no longer crowd the lists of the superrich, they do all right.

The committeewomen who run Chuterville today apparently see nothing much amiss. Telling each other to stay positive, they identify *negativity* as the town's big threat. Glorying in its history, its churches' Tiffany windows, its handsome (if bedbug-infested) public library, they keep busy with things that don't much matter, and every Saturday congratulate one another on the *Chronicle*'s editorial page for doing them: "Roses to the volunteers of the Hospital Auxiliary silent auction!" "Roses to the D.A.R.!"

Meanwhile, every summer Chuterville stages a comic melodrama in the piano-factory ruins to commemorate the women's temperance crusade that helped tame liquor's ravages on the town. How everyone roars with laughter at Demon Rum!

No one thinks to update the pageant to heroin. After all, to speak of heroin would smack of *negativity*.

Also, so far nobody finds heroin very funny.

## 12.

ADAM SNUFFED OUT a cigarette with his idea of the day: "Let's do Griggs."

"Good idea," said Jordan, and went to the window. The old man's rusty Cavalier was parked at his trailer three lots down. "He's home. Reds?"

The last reds.

Jordan drank some water, washed his face, brushed his hair, and found a Pop Tart. Adam chewing the larger half, they walked out.

A trailer park's like any small town, but more so: Everybody follows everybody else's comings and goings and speculates about them. Hitting a Shady Acres neighbor carried an air of desperation, but who would dare snitch on them? Adam felt armored in a cloak of invulnerability. For his part, Jordan looked distant and remote.

At Griggs's door Adam whispered, "Knock."

Jordan knocked and stood aside expressionless, nonchalantly putting his hands in his pockets.

Nothing.

"Again."

Knocking, Jordan called, "Hello, Mr. Griggs? It's Jordan? Jasmine Stocker's nephew?"

There was a stirring and a shuffle. Locks unsnapped and a wraith appeared through the screen door, a shaky hand opened it and a scowling white head pushed out.

— *JUNKIE, INDIANA* —

Jordan stepped up past the old man, too late seeing the gun come up in his other hand. But Jordan loved those moments, by nature unpredictable, where time slows up. Managing to wrest the gun from Griggs, he sent him sprawling. There was a *cra-ackkk!* as he hit the floor.

Adam closed the door. The old man was groaning, so he silenced him with a kick. There was a smell.

"Shit his pants?"

"Think it's the cats," Jordan said. He could see half a dozen cats; half a dozen visible meant a dozen invisible. The smell, compounded of ammonia and feces, was nasty. "Is he dead?"

"He'll be fine." Adam meant that nothing more was required of them. With pleasure he remarked of the automatic Jordan was holding, "That's a Smith & Wesson!"

"That's good," said Jordan. Already their venture had paid off.

Adam began searching one side of the trailer, while Jordan did the other with the blank expression he assumed when shopping.

Opening a kitchen drawer, Jordan found the Brownings. Pulling open a hutch, Adam found the shotguns and 30.06 rifles. Jordan found the Glocks, the Colts and the Walthers, Adam the Mannlichers, Remingtons, AK-47s and AR-15s.

"Holy shit," they were murmuring reverently. Their highest hope? Finding $100 in the freezer, where in fact they found *$400*.

In the bathroom Jordan paused to pet a tabby—after the shock of strangers' entry, the cats were beginning to relax—and pulled back a towel.

"Adam, got to see this!"

Coming in, Adam laughed at the sight: A loaded Luger lay rusted by cat piss into orange immobility.

They wrapped their haul in sheets and blankets and ferried it back to Jasmine Stocker's. Thoughtfully, Jordan left the old man's door open so his cats could escape. Griggs, breathing raspily on the floor, wouldn't be feeding them for a while.

Cordelia, seeing through her weepy scrim of spider webs the boys vanish into Jasmine Stocker's, went outdoors and tried to catch cats standing about stunned at the scope of the world. Most eluded her or clawed their way out of her arms, but she managed to deposit four in Fewkes's shed.

Then she walked to the Village Pantry and used the pay phone to call the police and alert them to the break-in.

Meanwhile Adam and Jordan found they'd piled up 31 guns, long guns and handguns alike. The Luger Adam placed on Jasmine Stocker's coffee table as a hostess gift—a conversation piece like her brass-filigree bong. Their haul meant they could stay high almost forever; so they were assuring each other when the first cruiser pulled past to Griggs's.

Smuggling some pistols to the Honda, the boys drove to their favorite pawn shop. But when Adam waved a 9mm at him, the proprietor, despite a palpable longing, refused even to look at it.

"Can't do it, guys," he told them. "Any idea of the paperwork?"

But across the state line in Sidestep they found a more accommodating dealer who bought two automatics, though Adam fretted they'd let them go cheap.

On the way home they stopped by East Side Orrie's. Keeping the motor running and looking tough, Adam dispatched Jordan across the street with a fistful of cash, which appeared to mollify Orrie.

Off they went to Dopeman's. Amused, he accepted a Beretta in exchange for supplies.

They returned home to hear from Jasmine Stocker that an ambulance had carried Griggs off and that the police, after seizing several guns and cats from his trailer (turning over the latter to Animal Control), had knocked at doors, including hers. But she didn't tell them anything; indeed, knew nothing.

She did exclaim at the cats suddenly roaming Shady Acres. Already a cop car had run one over. Adam went out and swung it by its tail into the gorge. Another, hit by a pickup, had crawled off the road with an eyeball hanging over its cheek and taken an hour to die. He disposed of that one, too.

Stalking a black cat, Cordelia appealed, "Adam, help me catch Mr. Griggs's cats?"

He laughed, and went in to get Jordan; time to pick up the babymama.

As they drove out, without knowing it they killed that black cat. It was crouched under a car, fearfully regarding *Cord* as she hurried to the rescue, and as the Honda passed leapt blindly into its tire. Head crushed, it sprang three feet into the air, then two feet, then a foot, then fell over dead.

Crying, Cord picked it up and carried it, dripping blood and matter, into the woods.

## 13.

THAT EVENING, Adam and Jordan were alone in the trailer, high and savoring the prospect of getting higher in any of several delectable ways, when they saw Cordelia walk past in the dusk, a tiger cat looking out alertly from her arms.

"Get her in here," said Adam.

Jordan went to the door and called, "Hey, Cord!"

With a jerk the tiger ran off.

"Hi, Jordan."

Smiling irresistibly, he said, "Come inside a minute."

Cordelia stepped up inside, but was taken aback at sight of Adam sprawled on the couch, legs spread, foot tapping, one hand behind his head, a joint in the other.

"Have a seat, Cord," he said easily, and inhaled. She took the scratchy green chair. In the ghost of a voice he offered, "Want a hit?"

Just to be polite, she inhaled with a wet sucking sound, then passed it to Jordan, standing beside her chair.

"So what went down today?" Adam asked.

She was sitting up straight, not against the chair back. She noticed the Luger but didn't say anything about it.

"Well, police got here half an hour after you guys came out of Mr. Griggs's trailer."

The boys froze. Finally Adam asked, *"And—?"*

"Ambulance came and took Mr. Griggs away. Cops were in there a long time, then they talked to people. Not me, though."

"How'd you get so sexy?" asked Adam.

"I don't know."

Jordan sat down on her chair arm and, smiling, pushed fingers through her hair as she looked up at him.

"You're so pretty, Cord," he told her.

"Thanks," she said, blushing.

Adam asked, "You red-haired all over?"

"I don't know."

"Who called the cops?"

"I did," she answered. "Didn't tell them who I was, though."

They were startled. Jordan said, "Oh, *Cord,* you shouldn't call the cops, not *ever,* not unless your trailer's on fire."

"Jordan, you should stay away from Adam. He uses drugs." The boys *laughed!* "I don't mean just weed."

"How do you know?"

"I just know."

"But he doesn't, you see, just a little grass, sometimes a tab or two."

Adam leaned forward. She shrank against the chair back.

"But really, Cord, what I do or don't do is *my* business," he told her. "Call the cops, you're stepping on *my* business. Bad things can happen."

He opened his hand to show sincerity, but spoke indignantly. It didn't matter that her calling the police led to nothing, he felt his invincibility infringed, rattled, disrespected.

"Tell them we were in his trailer?" Jordan asked.

"No. I'm no snitch."

They considered for a minute.

"Those lips?" Adam remarked. *"Push here for fun."*

*"Stuff me, please!"* said Jordan. "Have a boyfriend?"

"No."

"Want to be *my* special friend, Cor*dee*lia?" he offered, dropping his shoulder.

She touched her hair, with a jolt encountering his fingers.

"Would you like that, Cord?" Adam asked. "Be Jordan's special friend?"

"Maybe. Can you help me get Mr. Griggs's cats?"

"Any time, Cor*dee*lia," said Jordan. "Except right now we're busy."

"Got to go," she said, standing up.

"See you later, Cor*dee*lia."

They watched her chase a calico that fled in an urgent, low-slung run.

"Think we can trust her?" Jordan asked.

Adam snorted.

"Can you trust anybody in this world?"

## 14.

GRIGGS CAME HOME from the hospital with no memory of what happened, though he was not known to answer his door again. A few times he stood on the steps and called to his cats, but none responded beyond high-stepping along the edge of the woods, ears twitching.

Cordelia did her best to rescue them. She placed cardboard boxes stuffed with rags under various trailers so they could at least sleep dry and warm if they chose and, until Fewkes protested, fed them whatever she found in the refrigerator.

Soon they were following her schedule, showing themselves between trees or coming out from beneath trailers when she brought food around. At first they required her to retreat before they would advance, but day by day suffered her to come closer. Sometimes she scooped one up and tried to carry it to the shed, but usually it flurried out of her arms.

The crux was that, with so many to feed, Cordelia needed money. Fewkes told her he'd pay her to help him scrap, so she did it, sitting beside him as he took the Ranger down the alleys every morning.

That made Fewkes happy. He enjoyed her company, enjoyed passing on his skills, sharpening her eye for the value of detritus. Every 20 yards he dispatched her to go get that lamp base or check out the recyclables. For him, scrapping never ceased being fun. He had his rivals, to be sure, with whom he exchanged clipped and guarded waves as they pushed grocery carts down the same alleys or came at him in rustbucket pickups (Fewkes never the one to back up), but he scorned them as being, for the most part, *junkies*. For a time, Cordelia thought she and her dad were *junkies*, too.

Fewkes found joy as well as profit in coming across stuff before anybody else. He never knew what he'd find. Astonished him that the average householder couldn't be bothered to haul his own dead fridge down to Recycling for a good $40. No, they put it out for him, and Cordelia proved as useful in helping maneuver such prizes into the truck as in diving for beer cans.

On the way home, she bought cat food at the farm store.

Though Cordelia experienced anxiety in caring for her cats — those in the shed contrived to escape, all but the fat one — she found deep fulfillment also, lying on the grass as cats roosted near by bathing themselves or looking at her speculatively.

But the cats got on Fewkes's nerves, and he hated seeing Cord spend all her money on them. One day when she ventured to the library to page through cat books, he took his deer rifle and shot two of them — only two, the rest took off running, not to reappear for days, and he spared the one in the shed. Though curtains twitched, no one came outdoors to object as he threw the bodies into the gorge.

Then for days Cordelia went around Shady Acres and as far as the bridge calling for them. How she could tell them apart, much less have come up with names for them, Fewkes had no idea.

## 15.

WITH SELF-CONGRATULATORY FANFARE, the trustees of Squire Hospital donated their abandoned facility to the City of Chuterville, even staged a ceremony in front of it featuring a ribbon and giant cardboard pair of scissors.

The city fathers were ecstatic, confident developers would take the old hospital off their hands at a high price and put it on the tax rolls to boot: Was it not perfect for a nursing home? Retirement community? Residential school or treatment facility? Condos?

Once while Fewkes's arms were full of pipes he had to flee an official party coming through.

But by that time the old hospital had ceased to be his private preserve; rivals daily made raids on it. Water stood in the basements, tendrils of mold embroidered the walls, stalagmites of asbestos grew beneath broken ceiling tiles and crumbling pipe wrappings. Also, it turned out that for a century everything from kerosene to radiological waste had been dumped on the grounds. Those the city lured to assess the site's potential went away boggling at the expense of cleaning it up.

On the Fourth of July, Fewkes easily weighed down his truck with hospital metal and—the scrapyard closed for the holiday—on impulse on his way home swung into Continental Fixtures, nudged under the roof sawtoothed with broken skylights and stomped on the accelerator. Angled sunbeams dancing, the concrete pad offered a half-mile speedway. He had to swerve around puddles and a campfire tended by homeless men, but his Ranger achieved 75 m.p.h., if with a shimmy, by the time he burst out into the clear and had to brake hard so as not to hit the Chuterville Police cruiser sitting there.

He managed to miss it, but the cops arrested him anyway, for trespassing and for theft of the copper and steel in his truck bed. Unfair; it came not from the factory but the hospital.

But that fact Fewkes didn't volunteer.

## 16.

THAT DAY Jordan was lying outdoors in Jasmine Stocker's plastic-banded chaise lounge, shirt off and eyes closed, square in the middle of a cylinder of sunshine. Premature burps of celebration were going off all over town, stray cherry bombs and bottle rockets. He was waiting for Adam to wake up and tell him what they were doing that day.

Not much, he guessed. The boys were selling a gun or two a week, so could get high every night without having to worry about tomorrow. Adam took care of his remaining customers, too, making deliveries after getting the babymama home; that helped keep the party going. Two days earlier, they'd found a taker for an AK and—icing on the cake—come home to find Jasmine Stocker arrested "shopping" for dinner at Kroger. The trailer had been theirs since.

Jordan opened his eyes and watched clouds moving smartly eastward. The pressure exerted by their puzzle pieces slipping past delighted him, made him feel he was flying, infused him with that sense of well-being that comes from a sound chemical basis.

Horny, too. He got up and went indoors.

Adam, left logy and a mite confused by his night, sat smoking at the Formica kitchen table. Jordan embraced him from behind, gingerly placing his cheek against his cousin's.

"Off, man!" Adam muttered. "I want *cunt*."

"Me, too," Jordan said, disengaging.

"Worried about Cordelia," Adam said. "Even if she didn't snitch about Griggs, she *could,* and she's so *dumb,* land us in jail without meaning to. Just say the wrong thing to Fewkes or *anyone.*"

"So?"

"So we should do something, shut her the fuck up. Perfect time, with daddy away."

"Talk to her?"

"Oh, yeah, *talk*," Adam said. "No, something so she knows not to fuck with us."

"*Mmm?*"

"Don't mean *hurt* her, just have some fun." Blowing smoke, Adam scrounged in his wallet for a selection of blues and reds. "Up for that? Horny? You know she likes you, man—*loves* you."

"*Hell*, yeah!" said Jordan, swallowing pills.

"Catch her, she come by."

"'K," said Jordan and, bumming a cigarette, went outdoors to lie in the sun again and enjoy his renewed buzz.

Later, hearing Cord call, "Here, *kitty, kitty*," he looked up to see a white cat trotting away.

"Hey, Cor*dee*lia."

"Hi, Jordan."

"Come inside, something I want to show you."

"What is it?"

"Come on, I'll show you."

He got up smiling and held the door. She hesitated, then trailed indoors.

Sitting down on the unmade pullout, Jordan patted the blanket next to him. Cord sat down, folding a leg beneath her.

Adam came in from the back and sat down on her far side, asking, "How's it going, Cord?"

"Fine." She scrunched closer to Jordan.

"Listen," went Adam, "you a good kisser?"

"I don't know."

"Bet you are," Jordan said. "Those poufy lips?"

He put an arm around her, sniffed at her hair and licked her ear. Seeing her think, *I'd kiss you, Jordan,* he leaned in, pressing his naked chest beaded with sweat against her. Her lips on his were jumpy as hummingbirds.

For Jordan the scene was familiar, Adam using him to rope in a girl for sex. When he was younger, Adam and whatever girl he was with would do things to him, make him respond, grunting, beet red, desperately embarrassed but desperately excited too, while they fiddled and giggled. Wanting only Adam, he often got more of him in such situations than any other. Jordan never had sex with girls except for his cousin's sloppy seconds.

He kissed Cord again, while Adam canted his legs across hers and shoved an arm over her shoulders. Jordan tried to French-kiss her, but she turned her face and in her high little-girl voice said briskly, "Oh well, guys, got to go feed my cats."

She tried to get to her feet, but couldn't. She was stuck.

"Hang on, Cor*dee*lia."

"*Guys!*"

Jordan pulled at her hair, absorbed in admiration. Adam joined in, kissing it and his cousin's fingers. Grabbing Cord's hand, he tried to force it to his crotch, but it traced a butterfly's flight in the air and didn't land.

"*Guys!*"

"Dye job?" Adam asked.

"Definitely," said Jordan.

"No, I don't dye it," she said. "Guys, come *on!*"

"No, Cord, *you* come on," Jordan said with sudden roughness.

She looked in appeal at Adam but, finally jamming her hand into his groin, he just leered. Jordan began working her top off. Shocked, she breathed out a treble cry of resistance.

"Cord, help me out here," Jordan appealed.

"Jordan and me, we do *everything* together," Adam told her.

"Guys, *no!*" she said. "Jordan, *don't!*"

A FEW MINUTES LATER, she was crying bitterly and still kicking and punching, the effort nullified by the boys' weight, when Jordan gasped to Adam, "You're up."

"*I* don't want your sloppy seconds," said Adam. "Did you like that, Cord? Course you did, way you've been asking for it?"

He went off to find a cigarette.

"Now you're a woman," Jordan told her brusquely as he pulled up his jeans. Faced with the empty plinth he'd had a bad moment but, bent on pleasing Adam, he'd done it—popped her cherry. Now he tossed clothes at her that she clumsily pulled on. "Had our fun, but you better not tell."

"Not one word to *any*body *ever*," Adam added from a doorway. "Or *else*. Got me, Cord?"

Cordelia stumbled outdoors and headed towards her trailer, but sheared off, weeping, to the shed to visit her fat cat.

## 17.

FEWKES'S STAY AT the Main Street Hotel was only overnight. They shooed him out at 5:00 the next morning, warning him to stay off private property. He agreed, though sassing under his breath, "*What* private property? Belongs to Chinamen now."

He trudged home through the dawn. His first arrest; bitterly humiliating. His mug shot showed him with enormous sad eyes. Once home, soon as he could disentangle himself from Cordelia, he crashed.

Around noon, he woke up, got some cash—the check given him when he got out, representing what his wallet held at his arrest, being of no immediate use—and drove to the Village Pantry, where he spent a dollar on a glass rose from the box beside the register. He yearned for nothing but oblivion.

Unasked, the cashier also put a Brillo pad in the paper bag.

He bought his rock from a guy on a scooter in the parking lot.

Seeing him blow the tube's rose into the grass as he walked up his trailer steps, Jasmine Stocker, herself just home from jail, called from across the way, *"Fewkes!* Want some company?"

Hadn't occurred to him but, hand on doorknob, he turned and nodded: Yes, he *did* want company. Skanky Jasmine Stocker might be, and skanky during their thing a few years back, but he remembered her from junior high, too, the first girl in school with breasts; also knowing and reckless.

They retreated to his bedroom, where they smoked crack filtered through Brillo, the lighter *clicking, clicking, clicking,* the rock *glowing, glowing, glowing;* then *fucking, fucking, fucking* to get the reek of jail off.

After that he and Jasmine Stocker were together.

A week later a judge who had some sense of criminal priorities dismissed his case.

## 18.

CORDELIA WAS CRADLING a feisty young tom one day six weeks later when Adam and Jordan came out and tumbled into the Honda.

Jordan called, "Hey, Cor*dee*lia."

She ignored him, stepping into the trees and telling the tom, "We don't like you any more, Mr. Jordan, do we?"

Clearly Adam wasn't fit to drive; he hit a trash bin, making both boys laugh, and his entry onto the highway caused a screech of brakes.

Cord was having another day of heartache. To do your best for homeless cats is to live in perpetual pain. Despite her best efforts, they were constantly fewer; she was mystified and hurt. She put out food and water, petted those who would allow it, cradled those who let her. Still, one or two stole away or got run over or *something* every week.

And this with waking up sick every morning, bent over in her room (radio loud) vomiting into her wastebasket. She took Health in school, she knew what was going on.

Somewhere she'd seen a drawing of a homunculus, a miniature adult wearing a suit, tie and bowler hat—and an umbrella, she thought?—upside down in the womb. Whatever that may be, it wasn't a *baby*. It was an unwelcome reminder, a memorial to pain, anyway not *hers*.

"Something happened, Daddy," she longed to say, "but it's not *mine*. He put it in me, and if it gets bigger, it'll *kill* me."

She wanted to say this even kneeling next to him on the sidewalk in Louisville, pleading with women not to end their pregnancies. She wasn't troubled by any inconsistency, only by having to carry a child without her consent.

Of course she didn't tell Fewkes anything; he would be no help. She just went on, every day a reprieve in that things went on as they had the day before.

But also every day she knew moments of paradise, too, given her by the cats—miniature eternities of heaven sitting on the grass in the sun while around her they napped or rolled onto their backs or washed each other's faces.

The fat one in the shed had a litter of four kittens a couple of weeks after the Fourth, and Cord spent hours watching them bob against their mama's belly. Mama purred raucously while watching Cord with eyes of defiance.

Today, a hawk's wingspread inscribed against the sky, for the first time one by one Mama carried her kittens out of the shed and deposited them in front of Cordelia. For half an hour she proudly oversaw their play on the grass as they built themselves into pyramids, trading the topmost position with squeals of protest.

Then one went off in a wobbly, mad, determined kitten dash that made Cordelia laugh out loud.

In a trice the hawk dropped from silent orbit and grabbed it.

Despite Mama's instantaneous attack, that out-of-luck kitten was *gone*.

It was horrible. Cord packed the others safely away again, Mama yowling, and went for a long, moody walk along the gorge trail.

A few days later, the littlest kitten, a black-and-white, went missing. Cordelia was frantic with worry until she saw it standing at the edge of the woods. But it wouldn't come near and, when she went towards it, put back its ears, stretched out its paws and leapt into the gorge, a coyote-size snack. She couldn't get to it.

She was heartsick, but at sunset, while she forlornly set out food for the others, the kitten reappeared at the treeline. She sidled around and again gave chase. As before, it ran, its tiny body stretched rampant, but this time it ran in the other direction, into the middle of the loop where the tall grass proved too much for it and it ran to exhaustion in slow motion. It lay heaving its ribs when Cord scooped it up.

"This one's for me, Mama," she called, and smuggled the kitten under her shirt into her room.

There, as she fed it, it looked up at her with adoration. After going to the bathroom on her dirty laundry, it licked itself clean on the windowsill. At bedtime it stepped confidently into her arms and, resting its chin on hers, purred itself to sleep.

She named it Patchy; she and Patchy were bonded forevermore. He was the kitty of her heart.

## 19.

NO ONE SUSPECTED that anything had happened to Cordelia. She confided only in the cats; their sympathy helped, even as their numbers continued to decline—in one week, Ronnie and Smokey vanished, and then Mama disappeared.

Alerted by vultures circling over the loop, Cord found a pile of guts next to scraps of Mama's fur. Next day out of the corner of her eye she saw a small tan dog loping through Shady Acres. Turning her head fast, she freeze-framed a coyote. Yelling, she gave chase, and it fled. Fortunately the surviving kittens continued to play safely around the shed.

With no inkling of trouble, Fewkes followed routine. His evening ritual was to lounge on the frayed loveseat with beer, dinner, dessert and watch TV. That was when he felt happy, his premium-cable package and 46-inch screen carrying him securely along until bedtime. It was a tight squeeze on the loveseat now with Jasmine Stocker, but he liked being wedged between daughter and fiancée, rapt by *Duck Dynasty*, *Pawn Stars*, *Ice Road Truckers*, *Dog the Bounty Hunter*, sometimes, for Cordelia's benefit, *Animal Planet*, for Jasmine Stocker's, HGTV.

But suddenly Cord refused to watch TV. One Sunday evening while Jasmine Stocker comfortably remarked of a *Property Brothers* kitchen, "Hate the backsplash!" Fewkes at intervals was calling, "Cord, honey, we're in here!"

"Busy, Daddy." Busy petting her secret Patchy, busy ignoring *him*.

Fewkes finally padded down the hallway.

"What's wrong, babe?"

"Nothing," she called through the door.

"Save babies tomorrow?"

"Sure, Daddy."

All he could do was return to the living room.

"Love the crown molding!"

Next morning they were on the sidewalk, Fewkes in a hat and Cord slathered with sunscreen. Mutely they implored the women who passed not to enter what Father Loomis called "the blooditorium." But they did, every one of them.

Cord was squinting against the sun, her eyes a smear of blue, when a car came up and stopped. Motor chugging, it stood for a minute — then drove away.

Tearing off his tape, Father Loomis led the cheers, booming, "We just saved a baby's *life!*" Added Fewkes, "And a mother's *soul!*"

Smoking against the wall, Fewkes was still enjoying the triumph when another car came up. He flicked his butt away and assumed the position — clapped tape to his mouth, sank to his knees and implored the heavens; knees sore, but offering up the soreness.

Hands cupped, Cord looked a little funny as she drilled the girl walking past. The girl's companion, hand at her waist — surely her mother — looked warm and supportive.

So what happened next made no sense. Ripping off her tape and jumping to her feet, Cord entered the building behind them, the elder smiling as she passed off the weight of the black-glass door.

Walked straight into the *blooditorium.*

Instantly Father Loomis was at Fewkes's side. "She got a gun?"

"No," said Fewkes. "No way!"

"Then what the fuck's she up to?" the priest asked.

"Got me. Got me, Father. You want I should — go inside?"

"*No!*" Looking horrified, Father Loomis called, "OK, people, that's it for today! Thanks for coming, thanks for caring! Saved babies, I know it!"

They dispersed slowly, however, for the event was so

extraordinary. Fewkes's friends edged away, chary of him, and he was alone on the sidewalk when Cord came out, her face streaked with tears, the door this time held by a woman waving a sheet of paper who called, smiling, "Mr. Fewkes?"

"The fuck, Cord?"

"Daddy, they won't help me without your permission—I'm too young. You need to sign her slip."

Fewkes was stunned—his blood went iron. Arms around her, he started dragging Cord towards the Ranger.

"Please come inside, Mr. Fewkes? Mr. Fewkes, *please?*"

He pushed Cord into the truck.

"Daddy, they can't do it after 13 weeks. Has to be—"

"Shut your mouth, Cordelia," he said, shocked. "*Shut* it."

It was a tense trip home, their first without sliders or Cokes. Fewkes drove by habit—couldn't *see* a thing. But motion helped Cord screw up her courage.

"I love you, Daddy," she said as they passed the town of Correct.

"Oh, Cordelia! Love *you!*"

"Daddy, I need your help," she said in a small voice. "Also, she says we should report it to the police."

He took this in before responding, "Report *what*, Cord?"

She looked out the other side. "The rape."

"*What* rape?"

After a minute's silence, she said, "Doesn't matter, Daddy."

"Don't want people to *know*, do you?" Fewkes asked.

They got home in silence. Cord went to feed her cats. Fewkes informed Jasmine Stocker, who screwed up her mouth.

"Don't know who it could be," he concluded. "Doesn't even *know* any boys. Well, there's that one from school liked *her*. Went along worrying the bottom of his T shirt like a girl fussing with her skirt? But *rape? Him?*"

"Think her crush on Jordan got too much for her?"

"Oh shit." *One of the junkie cousins who sleep in the same bed?*

At sunset Father Loomis parked his black Infiniti and knocked. Jasmine Stocker fled for the back regions, but Fewkes placed the priest on the loveseat, in his honor turned off the TV.

"Unfortunate situation, Fewkes."

"Lord's sent it, we'll do the best we can."

"I'm sure you will," Father Loomis said, looking over at Cord and adding, low, "Look, but there's a place in Indy—*with* your permission, *and* your signature."

"*Place?*"

"Clinic. Got the form right here."

Fewkes was staggered. "Father, that's mortal sin!"

"Your call, of course, but delay is never good." When Fewkes said nothing, Father Loomis patted his side like a movie gangster. "Brought the Host, if you want Communion?"

Fewkes joined Jasmine Stocker in back.

Two days later, Cord somehow got that form to Indianapolis and presented it with her version of Fewkes's signature. But given her age they telephoned to double-check, and Fewkes dropped everything to go bring her home.

## 20.

AUGUST ENDING, the party was finally over. Adam and Jordan had swallowed, smoked, sniffed and injected every last gun, even those they meant to keep in case armed robbery beckoned—even the Luger. Waking up, they remained collapsed on the pullout. Neither felt at all well.

"Jesus," Adam complained, "don't we got *nothing?*"

"Nothing's what we got," Jordan confirmed.

Adam pointed two fingers at his temple and went, *"Pow!"*

A minute later, rubbing the back of his neck, head lolling forward, he said, *"Shit."*

Later: *"Thinking."*

Jordan got up to root around for something—*anything*—to help them adjust to being awake. In Jasmine Stocker's bedroom he found dried crumbs of weed, and they made do.

"Listen, my old man's house?" Adam said. "Let's go for it."

"His *house?*"

"Community Roses Dinner at the country club tonight, hundred bucks a head? They'll be there."

The annual dinner-dance was a highlight of Labor Day weekend.

"OK."

When past 6:00 that evening they drove out from under Shady Acres' foliage, heat hit like bricks to the head. Darkness was still hours off; the sun hung high and unmoving. The cousins felt sick, but anticipated feeling better later.

"So what're we looking for?" Jordan asked.

"Jewels, silver, guns, cash," said Adam.

"Power tools? Bet he's got great tools."

"Be ready to work, too, 'cause what we don't take goes in the pool."

Jordan laughed dutifully, but remarked, "Look personal."

"No, like a business beef. Dad pisses off a lot of people. Leave shit floating, look like a business beef. Never think of us."

"Whatever."

Adam laid out the plan. The house had no live-in help; his occasional surveillance established that. No obvious sign of security services or alarms, either, aside from the camera, almost too conspicuous to be real, aimed at the gatepost keypad. He doubted there were cameras inside, but to be on the safe side they would pull balaclavas over their heads and latex gloves on their hands and cut the power. There would then be no need for haste or worry. House should be empty until midnight; in and out in two, three hours, they'd be fine.

The evening began with a sign: As they went over a rise on County Line Road, a glossy Cadillac Escalade passed going the other way. Adam found himself looking down at its front seat.

"Holy shit, that was them!" he said, staring into the rearview.

"See us?"

"No," he answered. "Too wrapped up in each other."

In fact, impressed upon his retinas was a tableau luxurious and affectionate, a woman in furs (in 90° heat!) and big-city blonde helmet fondly engaged with the spiffily tuxedoed man behind the wheel. It tore at his heart.

The Honda arrived just outside camera range at the gate. Masked and gloved, Adam walked up to the keypad.

He left it to his fingers, though if the fingers failed they'd have a problem — have to leave the car where it might be seen, scale the fence, toss everything over it. His fingers tried the last four digits of his dad's social, plus asterisk. Nothing.

His dad's birth year, plus asterisk?

Nothing.

1234*?

No.

The year of his own birth — 1991 — and asterisk?

An accommodating click, and the gate rolled open.

"Holy shit!" yelled Jordan. The Honda passed through and the gate rolled shut, Jordan burbling with merriment. "How'd you *do* that?"

"Lucky guess."

Adam parked beside the six-car garage, out of sight of the road.

"*Jesus!*" Jordan said. The house's wings embraced a swimming pool whose terraces framed a vista of gardens, trees and distant hills. "Fucking *gorgeous!*"

Going up to the edge of the pool, irradiated in its glow, Adam spat in it, unzipped and peed. Jordan joining in, they vied for height and distance.

Fastening up, Jordan asked, "Where do we start?"

"Right here," said Adam, going over to a set of French doors. Locked. He picked up a wrought-iron chair and heaved it through in a splatter of glass. No alarm sounding, he reached daintily inside and turned the handle. "After *you.*"

They walked into a great room 15 feet high and *cold*. It was furnished with close attention to fabrics. Not to everyone's taste—Jordan liked it better than Adam.

"Gee, Dad, a little *frou-frou?*" Adam remarked, heading for the kitchen and garage.

"*Beautiful,*" said Jordan.

Maneuvering around convertibles and pickups, Adam found the breaker box and flipped the master.

Back in the great room at a bar flanked by mother-of-pearl columns they found Heinekens in the fridge. Taking them outside to the terrace they karate-chopped the caps off against a table edge.

"*Nice,*" Jordan said. "Really *nice.*"

"Old man does all right for himself."

They happily tipped their beers. Soon Jordan fetched more, with chips. They enjoyed the sight of each other hooded like terrorists.

"Live here if he let you?"

Adam snorted. "No *way.*"

Bottles tossed in the water, Jordan went off in search of silver and tools, while Adam went up the curving staircase. He almost tripped.

He found himself in rooms deeply carpeted, upholstered and aromatic. Going through double doors, he exclaimed at what he took to be the master suite, until drawers and closets proved empty. He decided it must instead be *his* room—what would have been his room. Next door he found a similar space, and next to that—twice the size, with a coffered ceiling—the master suite.

The bed was rumpled, as if mussed up just before departure. Adam took off his shoes, pulled back the covers, stepped up on the sheets, shoved down his pants, squatted and deposited a brick. Restoring the covers, he waded to one of the his-and-hers bathrooms to wipe himself. On the wall were framed photos of himself as a kid. He made to smash them, before thinking better of it.

The medicine cabinets yielded nothing but some Percocet; someone had been to the dentist. Soon he was feeling halfway decent for the first time all day.

Finding in his stepmother's dressing room a pair of diamond earrings left out in the open, he stuffed them in his pocket. From his father's he took a blue suit and pair of wingtips, regretfully leaving the wall safe behind; he couldn't open it.

After cruising through the rest of the upstairs—more bedrooms, a study and covered balcony, even another kitchen—he returned downstairs. This time he did trip, into a deep-piled rug. He and the suit were uninjured but indignant.

Jordan came in from the garage, flashlight in his mouth and arms full of power saws and drills, wearing gloves but no balaclava.

"Hell's your hat?"

"No camas, wight?" Jordan mouthed around the flashlight.

"Do we know that?"

Annoyed, Jordan dropped his load on the floor and pulled his balaclava back on.

Adam stashed suit and shoes in the Honda, already half filled with chainsaws and a leather case of sterling silver.

"Shit, no guns?"

"Big, locked gun safe. Can I take a look upstairs?"

"Knock yourself out."

While Jordan ran upstairs, Adam collapsed in a floral damask wingchair in the great room, energy sapped and volition vanished. The high satisfactions of burgling his father's house? Wasn't feeling it.

In frustration he bounced his head off the chairback. Found himself looking over the mantel at a mother and child in red that seemed familiar. Going near, he made out the signature — *Cassatt* — and lifted it off the wall. Didn't know, might be something; his dad came across funny things sometimes.

By the time Jordan came downstairs, Adam had also stacked a landscape signed Sawyier against two woodland scenes whose brass plates helpfully declared them to be by Harvey Joiner.

Jordan was mesmerized. "Adam, what a fucking palace!"

"Frilly as a whorehouse," his cousin said.

The sun was finally going, leaving behind a sky full of light that the pool placidly reflected. Cracking more beers, they drank them going through the rooms, including a screening room that yielded DVDs and game consoles.

Adam tossed his bottle in the pool.

"OK, now: Everything in the water. *Chop-chop.*"

Putting their heads down, they went to work. Adam came alive: His house, but not his house, he moved in, as it were, by means of unfurnishing it — furnishing it in reverse, trundling couches outdoors and across the terrace, Jordan on the other end, and heaving them into the deep end with mighty geysers.

They worked up a sweat dragging out chairs and tables and tossing them in, sloshing the flagstones; lofting cushions, lamps, platters; microwaves, toasters, espresso makers; bath towels, fireplace tools, Oriental runners, flatscreens, too. A surprising proportion floated — whole new furniture arrangements bobbed up and down.

Hands on hips, Adam said, "We'll call this the pool room."

Jordan said, "Only wish . . . "

"What?"

"We could stay the night. Just one."

"Well, we can't."

But Adam, popping a Viagra, did permit Jordan to suck him off poolside.

Reassuring each other they'd left no fingerprints, they finally carried bottles of Heineken and Maker's Mark to the car. Adam managed to leave rubber as they shot down the driveway to the gate.

Of course it didn't open.

"Crap," said Adam.

Back to the house, where he flipped the breakers again. The pool lights came up on a crazy lounge of bobbing stuff. This time the gate rolled open at their approach and shut behind them. There were no cars in sight.

"Can't believe you left a doodie in their bed," said Jordan, stripping off his balaclava. "Aren't you afraid of DNA?"

"Never been arrested."

They went home by way of Dopeman's; he liked an Xbox enough to get them very, very high. At Jasmine Stocker's, they hauled everything indoors and hid it the best they could. She was across the way at the crackhead's.

Neither knew anything about selling art or jewelry, but meanwhile the tools and silver—easy to fence—would keep them toasty for days.

And, Adam said with pleasure, he'd given it to his dad but *good*.

## 21.

THE BOYS WERE ARRESTED four days later. Enough of their antics had been caught on camera—discreetly placed, battery-powered miniatures, not to mention the gatepost one—that Adam's father was able to identify Jordan to the police as one of the burglars, and guessed the other to be his own son. But the police waited until they pawned the silver before picking them up.

Then units went out to Shady Acres and collected them and the remainder of the loot. Jordan they charged with B&E, burglary, possessing and passing stolen property and destruction of property; they had his face on camera.

They didn't have Adam's, so him they charged only with possessing and passing stolen property and with contempt—that is, nonsupport of his children; pressed by her parents, babymama #3 agreed to file on him. The police wanted to nail him for burglary, etc., too, but to do that would take Jordan's help.

Adam's mugshot captured the shock of his arrest—shoved in front of the camera at the instant the shutter clicked, earlobes and hair flared in the shove's direction, eyes peeping fearfully behind his specs.

Jordan's was that of a good-looking, if startled, teen, though he looked high, too. But it differed from his earlier mugshot; there his blue eyes looked out direct and bright. Now, wariness hooded eyes the color of gunmetal, and tension braced his lips and brow.

He was lodged in gen pop, Adam in an overnight tank, and they didn't encounter each other.

Jordan was repeatedly told that his cousin was making statements about him—blaming *him* for the burglary and other crimes. He didn't believe it, and had nothing to say in return. Anyway, he had his hands full being dopesick; diarrhea and vomiting filled his schedule.

So did they fill Adam's, but he was indeed talking about Jordan, encouraged by hearing from the lawyer his father sent that doing so could improve his situation, and finding that it helped take his mind off which end to aim at the toilet.

According to him, Jordan took the lead in burglarizing the house—himself but a reluctant helper, though he admitted to doing the driving. By way of deemphasizing that evening's acts, he had much to say about older crimes—narrated accounts of Jordan's robberies, burglaries, assaults, shoplifting, dealing drugs.

Gratified to be listened to, experiencing to the full the storyteller's joys, he felt purged by the telling—felt like the good citizen the detectives assured him he was. *Snitch?* Not at all; he was simply doing what anyone in his position would do. Isn't everyone responsible for himself? Shouldn't those who offend against society's good order be called to account?

Adam felt no guilt in ratting out his cousin. Jordan didn't have kids, after all, but he, Adam, had *four*, and what good would it do them to have their dad in prison?

Of course, a little voice niggled—and the lawyer confirmed—that if Jordan, too, were to talk, Adam might yet face trouble. But Adam had faith in his cousin's love for him, as well as in his father's reluctance to cause him problems (he thought sending the lawyer a good sign).

Hurst, again Jordan's public defender, was cautious in advising his client. Given that he was on probation, the best plea possible on the burglary-related charges would put him away for years; but in Hurst's experience, fathers seldom actually prosecute sons, and unless Adam's went after Adam, too, he expected the burglary charges against Jordan to go away.

However, he'd heard that Adam was providing information that might lead to new charges, so delicately suggested that Jordan review whatever he might know about Adam's criminal activity in order to be ready to counter them.

Jordan scoffed, "I'm no rat."

Assuredly, said Hurst, but if, for instance, Jordan could implicate Adam in selling drugs, it would undercut his cousin's credibility as a witness against *him*.

In the end, Adam's father didn't press charges, so the burglary counts melted away, leaving the cops with nothing on Adam but nonsupport. And so grateful was the prosecutor's office for what he told it about Jordan that it agreed to recommend a payment plan to the court whereby he could stay out of jail by making support payments of merely $80 a week.

The cousins were released from jail, unshackled in the lobby and Adam given a card listing his court appearance a few days hence. Jordan was a free man—for the moment; Hurst had guessed that he'd be freed on the old charges while warrants on new ones were perfected.

Each was shy of the other, for neither could be certain of the terms on which they met, but during the hike out to Shady Acres they thawed, and went into the trailer trading stories—how Jordan again had lucked out in not being sexually assaulted (he didn't mention several acts he preferred to think consensual), how glad Adam was that his dad kicked in to his commissary, thus sparing him the beans Jordan had to eat twice a day.

"Too bad they kept us apart," said Adam, "but the pigs were hoping we'd talk about each other."

"They wish!"

"Call my babymama soon's my phone's charged."

After a nap he left a voicemail with her, and at her lunch hour she returned the call, sarcastic about his wanting the Honda again after leaving her in the lurch the day of his arrest, and *No!* she wouldn't give it back.

"Sorry you feel that way," Adam said sweetly, and hung up. He found his key. "It's at Walgreens. Women are such shit."

"But they can't help it!"

It meant another hike, but the Honda sat in the parking lot. They drove it out.

Both feeling unwell, they agreed that what they needed was to get high. Adam even had a theory that their jailhouse detox meant getting high the *next* time would feel like the very *first* time.

At a stoplight he asked, "So, pigs talk to you?"

"What you mean?"

"Make a deal? Rat me out?"

"No," said Jordan. "Yeah, they suggested it, but I had nothing to say. *Nada.* You?"

"*Kidding?*" Adam asked. "Yeah, *wanted* me to, carried on like they *expected* me to, but *shit.*"

Both relaxed, to a degree.

"Now what?" Jordan asked.

"Watch and learn," Adam told him.

Pulling into an old customer's used-car lot, he trotted into the office shack and an extended negotiation ensued, with a few forays outdoors to look the car over.

The dealer explained that because of the lack of a title he'd have to lay it off out-of-state, hence couldn't pay much. It was a 14-year-old, high-mileage car not in the best of shape; still, a Honda. They made a deal. Adam pocketed $600, and was ecstatic.

Their next stop was Dopeman's.

Unexpectedly, a problem arose.

"Hey, man," said Dopeman.

"*Hey-a,*" Adam said, and showed his wad. "We want— Well, what's going?"

"What you mean, man?"

"Hydro to start, I think, and some uppers, and—hell, speedballs, right, Jordan? Go for it! And—"

"*Fuck!* Man, get out of here with that talk!" said Dopeman. "*Fuck!* Think I'm some kind of *dope* dealer? *Fuck!*"

He slammed the door shut.

"The fuck?" Jordan inquired.

"Get it?" said Adam. "Thinks we're wired up, made a deal with the cops."

"*Dick.*"

They went to McDonald's, had a good meal, but felt shaky even so. They were about past being sick, but the facts of Adam's court date and Jordan's uncertainty about what he might yet face made themselves felt.

"Don't feel so hot," admitted Adam. "We seriously need shit."

"Well, no one's going to sell to us," Jordan declared, proud of his insight.

"No, here's what we do: Go back to Dopeman's, knock on the back door, take off your clothes."

Oh, necessity! On Dopeman's rear porch Jordan stripped down to his boxers and knocked, but he had to wriggle out of his shorts, too, before Dopeman would let him in. He shook his ass at Adam and, looking like a stubborn little boy, walked naked into the house.

He came out ten minutes later so excited at first he forgot to get dressed. In each hand was a plastic bag weighted with things to get them high. Adam had urged spending every dollar, saying, "You never know." Now he said, "All *right!*"

They hiked home, where that night a strange thing happened.

Cordelia was petting Patchy at her window. The kitten arched his back urgently at every stroke and pressed his head into her palm. She looked up when Jasmine Stocker's trailer door opened and Jordan's hair caught the light. He eased outdoors and sat down on the steps. After sitting quietly for a few moments, he bent double, hugging himself and rocking back and forth.

Watching his seeming agony, Cord's anguish was acute, her heart constricting as she endured anew every episode of her crush on him. It wrung sobs from her.

Jordan's head bobbed in her direction, and he walked down the steps as she backed away from the window. But he just turned and peed in the bushes. He was high; it was an adventure in mushrooms that brought him outdoors.

Giving himself a shake, he went back in, slamming the door, and she knew him again for a careless kid best avoided.

## 22.

INEVITABLY THE DAY came when Fewkes lifted the cup of coffee Cordelia poured him and accused her, "You're showing."

"I noticed, too," put in Jasmine Stocker.

"I know it," Cord said, fussing with her top. "So what?"

"Now everyone will," grumped Fewkes. "Hey, birthday coming up, what you want for it?"

"What you won't give me," she answered.

She went outdoors to walk Patchy Cat around the loop.

He was the last of them; the others had vanished. Fewkes had long since discovered him in her room, but relented and allowed him to stay. Patchy delighted in walking with her every morning, running ahead from tree to tree, trailer to trailer, mewing, keeping his eyes on Cord as she called for the other cats. She hoped they'd left for better homes.

That morning Patchy didn't want to come back inside immediately, so she left him outdoors peeping through grass at some feeding sparrows.

A minute later Cord heard a kerfuffle. She burst outdoors and ran towards the shed, expecting to find Patchy either munching on a sparrow or bobbing at blades of tall grass, when she saw what she took to be wild turkeys flapping their wings at a puppy: It was vultures fending off a coyote from its own kill.

Her Patchy Cat lay stretched on the grass, his white streaked with red, mouth drawn back in a rictus, belly open and a vulture standing businesslike over him, pulling at an intestine while glaring at Cordelia through an executioner's red hood.

She picked up Patchy and took him inside the trailer.

That evening at sunset, Fewkes and Jasmine Stocker were absorbed in *Storage Wars* when Cord slid her window open, slipped out through spiderwebs' fingers and carried something towards the river.

The light was going fuzzy. Cicadas called. A lawn mower worked complainingly and a plastic bag caught in the upper reaches of a tree was flapping portentously. Although four bridges cross the gorge, people always jump from the one on U.S. 40. No one knows why.

Cordelia looked down at the water as she walked across. Swifts were making run after run at it, skimming for bugs. Then from beneath the bridge with unhurried and powerful strokes arose the blue heron, looking wider than the river itself. Her heart caught as it arced muscularly upstream, gliding downwards under the arch of the next bridge, small feet tucked neatly behind.

She watched it vanish, made a one-handed grab at the lamp standard beside her and swung up and over. Never looked down, never uttered a sound; gracefully done.

But the only witness shouted, *"Fuck!"*

Rescuers poured out of the firehouse across the gorge. They slipped down the slopes and splashed across the river, and found her broken and dead, her dead cat in her arms. Fireflies were lighting up. One would fly an upward arc and flash, instantly others nearby would flash. Somebody recognized her and went running for Fewkes.

A LifeLine helicopter landed at the clearing above the gorge, too late.

## 23.

ADAM AND JORDAN watched with indifference the panoply of disaster that surrounded Cordelia's death. The future as bleak as the past, they could yet—on the eve of Adam's hearing—keep themselves for the moment feeling fine.

Not that he enjoyed the justice system's contaminating touch, but Adam looked forward to getting court over and done with.

Jordan felt less peace. He didn't know what he faced, though he imagined that if Adam indeed had stood tough he could yet be all right; the cops couldn't have much on him unless Adam was making statements. But that Adam was getting off so lightly when they knew guys doing time for nonsupport made him wonder.

He asked once again, "You didn't tell them anything, did you, Adam? Got my back, right, bro?"

"Forever, man," said Adam, speaking from a distant place. "'Cept what the fuck could I do? Had you cold, man: *Cold*. Fucking *face* on fucking *cameras*?"

"Oh, *Adam!*"

"What would *you* have done, huh? Tell me that?"

"Adam, I didn't say a fucking *thing*, swear to God. What'd *you* tell them?"

"Don't worry about it," said Adam, drifting off. "*Que será, será.*"

After Adam fell asleep, Jordan kept up the party, with the result that when the phone alarm roused Adam, he couldn't awaken his cousin. He called 911.

For the second day in a row, a LifeLine copter landed beside the gorge. It flew Jordan to a hospital in Indianapolis.

He woke up 24 hours later. Such was his sky-high tolerance that though the drugs he took put him under, against all expectation they didn't kill him.

He didn't say thank you. After spending two nights chained to a bed, he was shoved into the pukey backseat of an old Crown Vic and delivered to Chuterville's jail and felony charges of possession, drug dealing, robbery, assault, theft and passing stolen property. His third mugshot showed a hard man easily 30 or 35; the grooves running from nose to mouth were pronounced. But the pain and fear spilling out of the eyes was youthful enough.

Meanwhile, Adam had to beg and borrow—at any rate, steal—to pay his first child-support installment.

Nuisance, hauling Jasmine Stocker's flatscreen to the pawnshop.

www.ingramcontent.com/pod-product-compliance
Lightning Source LLC
LaVergne TN
LVHW041631060526
838200LV00040B/1540